Spy Killer

SELECTED FICTION WORKS BY L. RON HUBBARD

FANTASY

The Case of the Friendly Corpse
Death's Deputy
Fear
The Ghoul
The Indigestible Triton
Slaves of Sleep & The Masters of Sleep
Typewriter in the Sky
The Ultimate Adventure

SCIENCE FICTION

Battlefield Earth
The Conquest of Space
The End Is Not Yet
Final Blackout
The Kilkenny Cats
The Kingslayer
The Mission Earth Dekalogy*
Ole Doc Methuselah
To the Stars

ADVENTURE

The Hell Job series

WESTERN

Buckskin Brigades
Empty Saddles
Guns of Mark Jardine
Hot Lead Payoff

A full list of L. Ron Hubbard's
novellas and short stories is provided at the back.

*Dekalogy—a group of ten volumes

L. RON HUBBARD

Spy Killer

Published by
Galaxy Press, LLC
7051 Hollywood Boulevard, Suite 200
Hollywood, CA 90028

Printed in the United States of America.

ISBN-10 1-59212-302-3
ISBN-13 978-1-59212-302-5

Library of Congress Control Number: 2007927545

Contents

Stories from Pulp Fiction's Golden Age

A ND it *was* a golden age.
The 1930s and 1940s were a vibrant, seminal time for a gigantic audience of eager readers, probably the largest per capita audience of readers in American history. The magazine racks were chock-full of publications with ragged trims, garish cover art, cheap brown pulp paper, low cover prices—and the most excitement you could hold in your hands.

"Pulp" magazines, named for their rough-cut, pulpwood paper, were a vehicle for more amazing tales than Scheherazade could have told in a million and one nights. Set apart from higher-class "slick" magazines, printed on fancy glossy paper with quality artwork and superior production values, the pulps were for the "rest of us," adventure story after adventure story for people who liked to *read.* Pulp fiction authors were no-holds-barred entertainers—real storytellers. They were more interested in a thrilling plot twist, a horrific villain or a white-knuckle adventure than they were in lavish prose or convoluted metaphors.

The sheer volume of tales released during this wondrous golden age remains unmatched in any other period of literary history—hundreds of thousands of published stories in over nine hundred different magazines. Some titles lasted only an issue or two; many magazines succumbed to paper shortages during World War II, while others endured for decades yet. Pulp fiction remains as a treasure trove of stories you can read, stories you can love, stories you can remember. The stories were driven by plot and character, with grand heroes, terrible villains, beautiful damsels (often in distress), diabolical plots, amazing places, breathless romances. The readers wanted to be taken beyond the mundane, to live adventures far removed from their ordinary lives—and the pulps rarely failed to deliver.

In that regard, pulp fiction stands in the tradition of all memorable literature. For as history has shown, good stories are much more than fancy prose. William Shakespeare, Charles Dickens, Jules Verne, Alexandre Dumas—many of the greatest literary figures wrote their fiction for the readers, not simply literary colleagues and academic admirers. And writers for pulp magazines were no exception. These publications reached an audience that dwarfed the circulations of today's short story magazines. Issues of the pulps were scooped up and read by over thirty million avid readers each month.

Because pulp fiction writers were often paid no more than a cent a word, they had to become prolific or starve. They also had to write aggressively. As Richard Kyle, publisher and editor of *Argosy,* the first and most long-lived of the pulps, so pointedly explained: "The pulp magazine writers, the best of them, worked for markets that did not write for critics or attempt to satisfy timid advertisers. Not having to answer to anyone other than their readers, they wrote about human beings on the edges of the unknown, in those new lands the future would explore. They wrote for what we would become, not for what we had already been."

Some of the more lasting names that graced the pulps include H. P. Lovecraft, Edgar Rice Burroughs, Robert E. Howard, Max Brand, Louis L'Amour, Elmore Leonard, Dashiell Hammett, Raymond Chandler, Erle Stanley Gardner, John D. MacDonald, Ray Bradbury, Isaac Asimov, Robert Heinlein—and, of course, L. Ron Hubbard.

In a word, he was among the most prolific and popular writers of the era. He was also the most enduring—hence this series—and certainly among the most legendary. It all began only months after he first tried his hand at fiction, with L. Ron Hubbard tales appearing in *Thrilling Adventures, Argosy, Five-Novels Monthly, Detective Fiction Weekly, Top-Notch, Texas Ranger, War Birds, Western Stories,* even *Romantic Range.* He could write on any subject, in any genre, from jungle explorers to deep-sea divers, from G-men and gangsters, cowboys and flying aces to mountain climbers, hard-boiled detectives and spies. But he really began to shine when he turned his talent to science fiction and fantasy of which he authored nearly fifty novels or novelettes to forever change the shape of those genres.

Following in the tradition of such famed authors as Herman Melville, Mark Twain, Jack London and Ernest Hemingway, Ron Hubbard actually lived adventures that his own characters would have admired—as an ethnologist among primitive tribes, as prospector and engineer in hostile climes, as a captain of vessels on four oceans. He even wrote a series of articles for *Argosy*, called "Hell Job," in which he lived and told of the most dangerous professions a man could put his hand to.

Finally, and just for good measure, he was also an accomplished photographer, artist, filmmaker, musician and educator. But he was first and foremost a *writer*, and that's the L. Ron Hubbard we come to know through the pages of this volume.

This library of Stories from the Golden Age presents the best of L. Ron Hubbard's fiction from the heyday of storytelling, the Golden Age of the pulp magazines. In these eighty volumes, readers are treated to a full banquet of 153 stories, a kaleidoscope of tales representing every imaginable genre: science fiction, fantasy, western, mystery, thriller, horror, even romance—action of all kinds and in all places.

Because the pulps themselves were printed on such inexpensive paper with high acid content, issues were not meant to endure. As the years go by, the original issues of every pulp from *Argosy* through *Zeppelin Stories* continue crumbling into brittle, brown dust. This library preserves the L. Ron Hubbard tales from that era, presented with a distinctive look that brings back the nostalgic flavor of those times.

L. Ron Hubbard's Stories from the Golden Age has something for every taste, every reader. These tales will return you to a time when fiction was good clean entertainment and the most fun a kid could have on a rainy afternoon or the best thing an adult could enjoy after a long day at work.

Pick up a volume, and remember what reading is supposed to be all about. Remember curling up with a *great story.*

—Kevin J. Anderson

KEVIN J. ANDERSON *is the author of more than ninety critically acclaimed works of speculative fiction, including The Saga of Seven Suns, the continuation of the Dune Chronicles with Brian Herbert, and his New York Times bestselling novelization of L. Ron Hubbard's* Ai! Pedrito!

Spy Killer

CHAPTER ONE

Dangerous Woman

THE water was black and the swim was long, but when a man is faced with death he does not consider odds.

Kurt Reid went over the side of the tanker *Rangoon* in a clean dive, cleaving the swirling dark surface of the Huangpu. The strong current swept him downriver toward the gaily lighted Bund. He did not want to go there. He knew that authorities would be after him like baying hounds before the night was out.

A shadow came between his half-immersed head and the glow. A sampan was sailing quietly through the gloom, its sculling oar stirring the thick black river.

Kurt Reid gripped the gunwale and slid himself over to the deck. The boatman stared at him with shuddering terror. Was this some devil come to life from the stream's depths?

"Ai! Ai!"

Kurt Reid was not too tired to grin. He stood up, water cascading from his black clothes.

"Put me ashore in the native city," he ordered in the Shanghai dialect.

"Ai . . . ai . . ."

"And chop-chop," added Kurt.

The boatman shriveled up over his oar. His eyes were two saucers of white porcelain, even his coolie coat sagged. He put the small craft about and drove it swiftly in toward the bank.

Kurt Reid grinned back at the looming hulk of the *Rangoon.* He raised his hand in a mock salute and muttered, "Get me if you can, gentlemen." He turned then and faced the nearing shore.

As he wrung the water from his clothes he discarded his memories one by one. As mate of the *Rangoon,* he had been known as a bucko sailor, a hard case who struck first and questioned afterward, renowned for a temper as hot and swift as a glowing rapier.

And the reputation had not helped him when the captain had been found dead in his cabin and when it was discovered that the safe was open and empty. Kurt Reid had been the last man to see the captain alive, so they thought.

Shanghai stretched before him, and behind it lay all of China. If he could not escape there, he thought, he deserved to die. His only regret now was the lack of money he had been accused of stealing. A man does not go far on a few American dollars.

But, unlike most American mates, Kurt Reid had been raised in the Orient and he knew the yellow countries and their languages. Although his quick temper had earned his many enemies among the Japanese and Chinese, he hoped to avoid them. By now several men would be advised of his arrest and before morning his escape would also be known. Many men would think that excellent news and hope that his apprehension would be speedy.

4

If necessary he could assume one disguise or another. His eyes were the color of midnight and his hair was even blacker, and the pallor of his face could be easily made saffron.

The sampan rasped against a float and Kurt Reid, throwing a coin to the boatman, stepped ashore into the din of the native city.

Rickshaws clanged, vendors yowled their wares, jugglers threw tops high into the air and made them scream. Silk gowns rubbed against cotton gowns, scabby slippers stubbed over jeweled shoes. The crowds in the curving streets blended into the democracy of China.

Kurt Reid, head and shoulders above the rest, shoved his way toward a tea house. There, he supposed, he could dry his clothing and get himself a drink or two. Confidently he picked his way, looking neither to the right or the left, paying little heed to those who stopped to stare at this black-clothed giant who left the cobblestones spotted with his dripping passage.

The tea house was set a little apart from the other structures which hung flimsily over the street. The tea house had curving corners to foil the devils and a floating banner or two in red letters and a whole row of paper lanterns.

Kurt entered and rolled back the clouds of blue smoke which hung between ceiling and floor. Black caps bobbed, gowns rustled. Tea cups remained suspended for seconds.

Kurt went to the back of the room and found the round-faced, slit-eyed proprietor. "I want to dry my clothes. I fell into the river."

The man opened up a small cubicle at the rear, clapped his hands sharply, and presently a charcoal brazier was placed on the floor.

Kurt shut the door and disrobed, hanging his black flannel shirt and his bell-bottom pants over a bench to dry. Tea was brought, but he waved it aside in favor of hot rice wine.

The clothes began to steam and the rice wine took the chill from his body.

All unsuspecting and feeling at ease, Kurt began to plan ways and means of getting into the interior and away from possible arrest.

If he could buy a gown from this Chinese and perhaps a few other things, everything would be all right. He could join some party of merchants and get away.

But his plans were for nothing. His clothing was soon dry and he dressed again, feeling cheered and optimistic. He clapped his hands for the proprietor, and when that worthy came, Kurt was startled by a woman who sat with her back to the wall, staring out into the milling street.

Kurt slipped a dollar bill into the proprietor's hand. He still studied the woman. She was obviously a Russian. Her face was flat, with high cheekbones, and her nostrils were broad. There was the slightest hint of a slant to her eyes. She wore a coat made of expensive fur, and a small fur hat sat rakishly on the side of her blonde head. It was not usual to find Russian women alone in the native city, especially Russian women who dressed so well.

"Who is that?" demanded Kurt.

The Chinese inspected the girl as though he were seeing her for the first time. "Name Varinka Savischna," he replied, stumbling over the unfamiliar vowels of the Russian name.

"But . . . a white woman in the native city . . ." said Kurt.

"Russian woman," grumbled the Chinese. "She brings trouble to me." He looked at Kurt's lean body and handsome, inquisitive face and then grinned.

As though the thoughts of the two men were projected to her, Varinka Savischna turned slowly in her chair, placed her arm idly against the table and tapped the toe of a fur-topped boot against the rough floor. The steam which rose from her cup of tea was not less illusive than the quality of her eyes. Casually, impersonally, she inspected the tall American. She drew a long cigarette from her pocket and inserted it languidly between her full, scarlet lips.

Kurt felt the magnetic pull of her personality, and he caught an uneasiness she did not display. She was signaling him somehow. He picked up a packet of Chinese matches from a table and went slowly toward her. Without a word he lighted her cigarette.

She touched a chair leg with her boot. "Sit down, American."

Kurt sat down. He had two thoughts in mind. This girl appeared rich and she might be in trouble. If he could perform some small service for her, he might gain materially as well appease the taste for chivalry which bubbled up inside him.

Varinka looked quickly about her and then leaned across the table, staring intently at him through the steam which flowed upward from her cup.

"You do not belong here, American."

"No, and neither do you," said Kurt.

"My messenger is late. Perhaps you have a moment's time to do a small favor for Varinka, eh?"

"Perhaps," said Kurt.

"This is a very important matter, American. If I can trust you to take a letter to— But then, how do I know that I can give you my confidence, eh?"

"Look at me and find out," said Kurt.

She drew a small envelope from her pocket and slid it face-down across the board to him. "I cannot take this myself. I have been waiting here for one who could, but my messenger did not come, and if they have caught him then perhaps you had better not stay with me too long. You understand, American? Tell this man that you have been of slight service to Varinka, and he will reward you."

"If you're liable to be caught," said Kurt, "let's get out of here."

"No, there is too much—" She broke off with a startled gasp. Her eyes flew wide as she looked at the door.

Kurt spun in his chair. Two men were there at the entrance, looking over the room. They were both Chinese from the North, tall and bony-faced. They wore black suits which had a suggestion of a uniform. Their hands were thrust deep into their pockets, as though they held hidden guns.

The pair saw Varinka and their glance steadied on her. They came slowly through the crowded room. The Chinese, knowing what to expect, dived sideways out of the line of fire. Kurt was rising slowly from his chair.

8

"No, no," whispered Varinka. "Let them take me. Take the letter and go while there is yet time."

The two men came on, skirting tables, eyes fastened upon the Russian girl. Kurt knew that he was in no position to involve himself in some political mess, but he was spoiling for a fight. He got it.

Kurt stepped out, away from the table, as though about to leave the girl and make his escape. The Chinese on the right shifted his glance, hesitated, and then started after Kurt. The other man walked on toward Varinka.

There was something horrible in the way the pair walked, something which suggested an executioner's keen blade or perhaps a firing squad.

Kurt stopped. The Chinese came on. Kurt began to advance. The Chinese hesitated briefly and started to pull an automatic into view.

With an ear-shattering yell, Kurt dived in toward the gun. The blunt muzzle swept up. Kurt's palm jabbed the slide back. The firing pin clicked a fraction of an inch from the cartridge.

Kurt swung his right. The Chinese was lifted up a foot from the floor. Bent backward like a falling tree, the man crashed into a table and went down.

The other man whirled about and whipped up his weapon. He fired, but the hand of Varinka was quicker than his trigger finger, and the shot furrowed the ceiling.

Kurt stepped within two feet of the big Chinese and swung. The fist connected with a crack louder than a breaking staff. Kurt swung again and the Chinese folded into himself with a grunt.

With an ear–shattering yell,
Kurt dived in toward the gun.

Varinka ran toward the entrance. Kurt paused long enough to pocket the two automatics and then he sped after her twinkling boots.

They raced up the crowded street, Kurt spilling the crowd to the right and left as a cutter's bow cleaves water. They dashed down a dark alleyway and through a garden.

Breathless, they paused in the shadow of a wall. The girl leaned her head back and peered up at the muddy sky. She was smiling.

"When . . . when Lin Wang . . . hears of this . . ." she chuckled. "How he'll . . . pant for vengeance. The pick of his Death Squad knocked kicking by one man!"

"Aw, they didn't know how to box," said Kurt, embarrassed.

"Ah, but they do. You, American, were glorious. But come, my fine white knight—let me dispose of this letter another way. A block from here I have another man, one I should have contacted first. Come."

They picked their way through the littered alley and soon came to a low door on which Varinka knocked. A small, shaved head was thrust fearfully forth.

"Ah, the white lady," sighed the Chinese with relief. "Tonight Sing was taken and made to talk—we are no longer safe here. I waited another hour for your coming, against my will."

"They made Sing talk?" said Varinka, growing pale. "Then he is dead."

"Ai, dead. Lin Wang's Death Squad strikes fast."

"But here, take this letter to the commander. I have not proof of it, but he will do well to watch Lin Wang."

"The commander left this for you," said the Chinese, handing out a slip of thin paper.

The girl pocketed the order, the door slammed shut. Varinka led the puzzled Kurt down another alley.

"You are in trouble," she said. "I might even guess who you are. Your name might be Kurt Reid?"

He blinked at her.

"And tonight, American, you found the cell door of the *Rangoon* mysteriously open?"

"Yes, how—"

"Never mind, American. Your destiny is written tonight. You can do one of two things. You can drift outward and try to lose yourself—which you cannot—or you can try to be of service to me."

"There's no decision to make. Whatever I can do—"

"Beware, think not fast, American. I am a dangerous woman."

Kurt laughed at her and followed her through the gloom.

CHAPTER TWO

The Russian Disappears

VARINKA SAVISCHNA took Kurt Reid through the back streets of Shanghai's native city to another garden. They entered through a small door and walked across meandering paths, past pools where stone storks stood in one-legged sorrow. Paper lanterns cast their gay reflection in the water and lit up well-tended beds of flowers. This was a spot of beauty in a squalid settlement, as unexpected as a warm house in the Arctic circle.

Through a broad blackwood door they entered a large, well-furnished room. The light was subdued, suggesting mysteries behind the walls and in the shadows. A thick Oriental carpet softened their footsteps.

Varinka made Kurt sit down in a long chair. She did not remove her coat. She looked about her with an air of worry. "She should be here."

"Who?"

Varinka did not answer that. She sat down and studied Kurt. "You have a reputation, American, one that I might be able to use if things go well. We know of you here in Shanghai and we know what happened to you. It will not be well for you to roam the streets of the city. Until I need you I shall have to keep you hidden. One flare of temper and . . . whack—off goes your head."

"You mean you—?"

"No, no," she laughed. "Not I. The authorities—and perhaps another. You must promise to stay here until I can tell you when to leave."

"Maybe if you let me in on some of this, I could help you better."

"No, I do not think I am at liberty to tell anyone."

"I trusted you," he reminded her.

"But my secrets are not my own. There is much to be done, American—things which are greater than ourselves."

"If this has anything to do with Russia—" began Kurt, suddenly waking up to the danger of his position.

"Hah, you think that I am a Russian spy, eh? But no, I am a White Russian. This has to do with China and Japan. Great forces are at work. You will undoubtedly know of them soon enough."

Kurt sat forward. He smiled, displaying close-set teeth in a scimitar's arc. "I have nothing to do but escape. The reason I talked to you at the tea house is easily enough explained. I thought I could do something for you and you could help me get out. But you seem to know more about the setup than I do. You seem to know more about me than my own mother. How is this?"

"We watch everything, American."

"And who do you mean by 'We'?"

Varinka stood up suddenly. She touched his shoulder lightly. "You want escape. Perhaps that will come too. But first, help me. Stay here until you are wanted. She will be here soon. You will wait for her."

Abruptly she pulled back his head and gave him a hard kiss upon the mouth. Before he could voice his surprise she stood halfway through another door.

"I hope to see you soon, American," she said, and disappeared.

He tried then to follow her, but he found that she had locked the door behind her. He tried another door and it, too, was locked.

Suddenly something like panic came over him. He was a prisoner again, and although his captor was fair, and although he had no definite reasons for alarm, the late brig sentence had given him a taste for freedom he never again would forget.

Kurt found that the windows had iron bars across them, though the bars were masked by carved sandalwood. He strode up and down the room. What a fool he was to let himself get taken in by a Russki spy! Perhaps she was even then going for the police—and it would be Chinese police, too. Not American or British. The *Rangoon* was under Chinese Nationalist registry.

"Whack—and off goes your head," muttered Kurt.

He found a decanter and poured himself a drink. Then, peering into the glass, he decided that even a decanter could not be trusted. He set the drink down untouched.

Funny girl, that Russian. She had kept him from questioning her by the sheer force of her personality. She seemed to have some numbing power over him which fell as tangible as a cloak.

He felt angry at that. It didn't make him feel strong or masculine. And now he was trapped again, waiting for . . .

What was he waiting for? What rubbish was that about

China and Japan? Maybe this girl had a need of him. Maybe he was supposed to strong-arm for her in her work. Maybe she had had him released and had had him trailed to that tea house.

And now that he thought about it, he had been released. Cell doors do not open by accident.

And that sampan had been handy, too.

But why should anyone take an interest in him? He wasn't anybody but a bucko mate off a coastwise tramp. Plenty of available white men could speak Chinese and Japanese and more dialects than he could.

He sat down in the chair again. Grinned, recovering his sense of humor. Here he was, and he didn't exactly mind after all. Hadn't the girl kissed him? Women didn't kiss you and then go find a guy who would cut off your head.

Or did they?

A light footstep brought him to his feet. A key grated in a lock and the door swung inward. Kurt, who had been expecting the return of the Russian girl, gasped in surprise.

"Anne Carsten!" exclaimed Kurt.

The woman who entered was slender, well poised and very beautiful. Her hair was light brown, matching her eyes. Her face was aristocratic and well molded. Her body was sheathed in a satin gown which whispered as she walked. She had the air of one who is born to command, but her eyes were kind and her smile was gentle. She gave Kurt her hands and looked at him for many seconds without speaking.

"I have not seen you for two years, Kurt," she said. "Since

that night you told me that you were just a bucko mate, destined for the sea, and left me so precipitately. Did I scare you badly, Kurt?"

Surprise still held him motionless. His mind went back to a sailor's holiday when he had been invited to a gay social function in the Concession. He had met this girl there, had met her amid the tinsel and pomp and dreamy music. Anne Carsten, then, had ruled the social world of Shanghai through the position of her merchant prince father, a man who had since died. Their interest in each other had been heightened by the romance of the night, until . . .

"I could have given you so much," said Anne, accusingly. "I could have made you a king of captains, but you were frightened, weren't you?"

Kurt laughed, embarrassed. "I didn't want to be known as Anne Carsten's husband. I wanted to be Mr. Reid, not Mr. Carsten."

"You told me that I had been made for silk and spice, that I belonged in luxury and that your path led through hardship, that you wanted your woman to be as bold as yourself. Silly thoughts, weren't they? But then, it might have been the music."

"Or your eyes," said Kurt. "You're more beautiful than ever. I've thought about you—"

"You never gave me another thought. Don't lie for the sake of gallantry. How handsome you are and how rugged. Then you were dressed in a tuxedo. I never suspected—"

"And now I'm a hunted killer," said Kurt with a twinge of

17

bitterness, dropping her hands and stepping back as though his presence defiled her. "I heard about your father. I wanted to return and tell you . . ."

Anne Carsten smiled again. "I see that you know my friend Varinka well. Look in the mirror."

Kurt wiped the back of his hand across his mouth. It came away smeared with lipstick. He had the good grace to blush.

"Tell me," said Anne, "do you love this Varinka now?"

"No, no," he replied hastily. "I only met her tonight. How is it that she comes here?"

"She is my friend. An exotic creature, isn't she? So mysterious. I never know when she will come or when she will go. But she is my friend, and whatever her business, my home is hers. Are you sure you don't love her now?"

"I respect her nerve," said Kurt. "But tell me what you're doing here, all alone in the native city."

"One cannot live cheaply in the Concession."

"Is it that bad? I thought your father had a great deal of money."

"He left little enough, Kurt. But somehow . . ." She moved closer to him and placed her hands on his shoulders. Her eyes searched his face for a full minute, and then with a sigh she placed her head on his broad chest.

He realized then that she was tired and worried, but he could find no words with which to comfort her. His own worries were forgotten for the moment. Funny how their paths would cross again after two years. Then she had been so arrogant, so satisfied with her station. And now she lived in the native city, probably broke, away from her friends.

She thrust herself away from him with a smile. "But then, you probably won't remember me tomorrow. You have Varinka to think about."

"No, listen, Varinka doesn't mean anything to me. She's a Russki. You don't marry Russkis. And besides . . ."

She laughed at his confusion and sank down in a long chair. However poor might be her pocketbook, she was rich in beauty and poise. Kurt felt a troubled stirring within him. He had come back to her and soon he would have to go away. To cover the thought he poured himself a drink and downed it.

"I can't stay," he said at length. "I'm outward bound—God knows where. They want me for . . . for a murder I didn't do."

"But I thought that you would stay for a little while. You are safe here. No one would dare molest me. You look haggard, in need of a rest. I thought—"

Kurt never knew what she thought. The great blackwood door rocked on its hinges and thunder rolled through the room. Kurt froze.

Anne Carsten stood up and motioned toward the door through which she had entered. The door shuddered and Kurt rushed into the other room and looked about him. He realized with a shock that there was no exit, unless one of the panels moved. He tried to find a compressed spring, but from the outer room he heard voices. Anne Carsten had opened the door.

Kurt stepped into a clothes press and tried not to breathe. If they knew he was here, then . . .

A booming Chinese voice said, "You have here a Russian woman. Varinka Savischna. Where is she?"

Anne Carsten's softer tones replied, "I know of no such woman. You must be mad."

"You think to fool the Death Squad, my lady? Oh, never fear, we respect the women of the Foreign Devils, even when they are not in their Concessions. But I must have this Russian!"

"There is no one here but myself," said Anne Carsten.

"I am sorry, but we must search."

Anne Carsten's voice was lost in the shrill babble of Chinese voices. From his place in the clothes press, Kurt saw men enter the bedroom. These men were not Southern Chinese. They were immense Northerners. They were all dressed in black, like so many oversized buzzards. They carried automatics in their hands and bayonets at their sides. Of the six men there, not one was less than six feet tall. Their eyes were flinty hard.

The two approached the clothes press. Kurt braced himself for inevitable discovery. The two jerked back the fine gowns.

Kurt, knowing that fighting was useless, nevertheless threw himself at them before they could set themselves. He rolled one back and sent the other reeling. He plunged out through the door and tried to get across the larger room.

He had a vision of a massive face before him. He struck, but his knuckles received the only punishment. Men dived in from all sides and pinned Kurt down.

The big one knelt on Kurt's chest and lifted his automatic for a blow. Anne Carsten screamed. Kurt tried to roll away. The big one thought better of it and stayed his hand. Kurt was helpless, and the others were swiftly binding him.

"For your knowledge," said this big one, "I am Yang Ch'ieu, captain of the Death Squad. Of course you know why we are here, and you know what is about to happen to you. My master, Lin Wang, sees over all and allows no evil to escape. You are being taken to him. If I have bothered this lady of yours, I ask her pardon."

Yang stood up. He looked like some animated dark mountain. His arms and legs were as big as tree trunks, and his head sat oddly small on his great shoulders. But his head, on closer inspection, proved twice as large as an ordinary man's. Yang weighed three hundred and fifty pounds, and none of it was fat. His expression was one of proud disdain. The five others showed cruelty, but not Yang.

They picked Kurt up, like so much straw, and started out. Anne Carsten cried out to stop them. Yang turned to her with a respectful bow.

"You cannot do this!" cried Anne. "He is an American. The United States—"

"Will be very glad to have him, madam. He is a murderer."

Anne Carsten looked beseechingly at Yang, and finding no hope there, stared down at Kurt. She touched his face lightly with her fingers.

"I . . . I hoped . . ." she whispered, "to see you . . . again." She was crying now. Kurt turned his face away.

The Death Squad carried their burden through the garden and through the wall, toward the headquarters of Lin Wang. . . .

CHAPTER THREE

The Confession

W HEN a man spends a month in jail, he is ready for anything, even murder. And murder was to be the task of Kurt Reid.

The first week he spent worrying. No one came to see him, no one advised him of the exact nature of his arrest, he heard nothing of the two strange women who had indirectly caused his incarceration.

A man can find a great deal to worry about when he is confronted with four yellowish walls and when the scurrying rats forbid his sleep. He was unable to pry information out of his black-uniformed guard.

In the second week he began to suspect the Russian Varinka Savischna. At the end of ten days he received a short note via the one window of the cell.

Kurt Reid;

I have tried to find out about your case, but I am afraid to take my information to the authorities, fearing that the affair aboard the *Rangoon* would also be brought against you. I have tried to bribe Lin Wang, but he will have nothing of it, saying that you are an enemy of China. If fate brings you back to me, I promise that our next meeting will be far better than the last.

Anne Carsten

There was some slight solace to that, and he found himself looking forward to seeing the girl—if and when—he ever got out. He began to dwell upon her beauty, upon the kindness of her eyes. He realized, then, that this was the girl he had always hoped to meet. His luck to meet her when he had to depart so abruptly. Sailor's luck!

He could not fathom Lin Wang's determination to keep him away from the Shanghai authorities. The fact was ominous. If Lin Wang merely wanted to do away with Kurt Reid, it would be more quickly done over the bar of justice—God knew that Justice had enough against the bucko mate.

He tried to piece together all he knew about Lin Wang, but that did him little good. Lin Wang was a general of high repute, shouting for China's freedom and waving flags and putting up a great show. China's traitors, so boasted Lin Wang, did not live long at the hands of his picked executioners, the Death Squad.

Lin Wang had long called down the ancient curses upon the head of invading Japan.

But Kurt Reid had no definite answer and when the month was out, curiosity overcame the fear of his first meeting with Lin Wang.

The soldiers in black came one morning and led him away. Between their files he was not much to look upon. His clothes were dirty and worn, he needed a shave, his hair was long and unkempt, but he walked with erect head and something of arrogance in his stride. He was thrust through the door of a small hut and made to sit in a chair against the wall. Men passed ropes through his arms and about his body and lashed him there.

For an hour he waited and then, amid great clamor, the door was flung back and Lin Wang came in.

One glance at the man sent a shudder of repulsion through Kurt. Lin Wang was small, hunched to one side, with a twisted back. He did not seem to have any neck muscles; his head sat rigidly upon his shoulders, pulled to one side. His face was deeply pocked, covered with yellowish scales which might come from some leprosy. Several great wrinkles lay like old scars against the cruel visage like ravines in a relief map. The wrinkles were filled with ancient poisonous dirt.

Lin Wang's hands were held up from his body as though he could not drop them. The fingers dangled limply, fleshless and thin, clattering nervelessly when Lin Wang moved.

But the eyes were the worst. They were not black, they were an unhealthy, mud blue color, like bichloride of mercury. The lids were half lowered over the protruding pupils.

"Kurt Reid, isn't it?" said Lin Wang with a rattle in his voice.

Kurt drew back a little and said nothing.

"Ah, so you do not like to look at me. No one likes to look at Lin Wang. But for all my looks, women sometimes smile. Could you smile, bucko mate, watching a beheading sword?"

"I'm laughing out loud," said Kurt, teeth displayed by his taut upper lip. "What do you want with me?"

"I will show you that, but first allow me to ask you a question." Lin Wang settled himself behind the crude desk and popped three black opium pills into his mouth, lowering his hands and letting the clattering fingers droop, eyeing Kurt with a twisted glance.

"You are very good-looking," commented Lin Wang. "The women, I presume, love a man as good-looking as you. Perhaps Anne Carsten, for instance. I have a feeling that it might give me pleasure to spoil those handsome features of yours, Kurt Reid, but nevermind, perhaps that will come later."

"What's the idea of bringing me here?" demanded Kurt. "You could have saved yourself the trouble by tipping off the officials over in the Foreign Concessions."

"Ah, you refer to that incident aboard the *Rangoon*, eh? With regard to that, Kurt Reid, allow me to state that I have gone to no little trouble for you. I have solved the murder aboard the *Rangoon*."

"What the hell?"

"You see? We might even be friends. But tell me, are you the Kurt Reid who spent his life here in China and Japan? Was your father a certain Frank Reid, a soldier of no little reputation?"

"That's right."

"I had hoped that I would not be in error. Then you speak several dialects of Chinese and Japanese as well?"

"I do," said Kurt.

"And you're the bucko mate with the quick temper?"

"I suppose so."

"Very well," said Lin Wang, with an air of finality. He turned to the black-uniformed Yang, captain of the Death Squad. "Bring that seaman in here, Captain Yang."

Yang's great bulk filled the doorway as he went out. Presently a hulking seaman was goaded through the door at the point of bayonets. The man was thick of body and small-headed. His face was unclean, and matted dark hair clung stickily to his half-naked body.

"Bonner!" exclaimed Kurt Reid, recognizing one of the *Rangoon*'s seamen.

"Bonner is right," said Lin Wang. "Then my men were not in error. I might mention, Kurt Reid, that I had a friend in the crew of the *Rangoon* who was willing to sell me this information at a price."

Bonner glowered at Lin Wang, and then saw Kurt Reid. He growled a curse and said, "What the hell do you want with me?"

Lin Wang smiled and the chasms in his face opened. A thin scale dropped from his face and he picked it up from the desk, breaking it with his finger nails.

"Bonner," said Lin Wang. "I believe you murdered the captain of the *Rangoon* and took a few things from the safe. My men found those things in your baggage when you jumped ship in Hong Kong."

"So that's where they went! Well, listen, yellow-belly—"

"I am doing the talking," said Lin Wang. "If you care to give me a written confession, you can remain alive. Otherwise—"

"Go to hell," said Bonner.

"Yang," said Lin Wang, "pin his body in a chair and bring me a pair of pliers. Any pair of pliers will do."

Bonner swore, but strong hands bent him into the chair and strong ropes held him down. He tried to twist free, but the black-uniformed men were stronger.

The pliers came. Kurt Reid watched with wide open eyes. Lin Wang rattled the metal in his shaking hand.

"Spread out his fingers," said Lin Wang, smiling.

Yang spread the man's hand flat against the arm of the seat. Lin Wang's smile broadened. The muddy blue eyes lighted up. A desire of cruelty, heightened by the fact that he was a crossbreed between some unknown race and Chinese, made Lin Wang chuckle.

The pliers swept down with a click and fastened upon Bonner's index fingernail. The pliers jerked back, blood spouted. Lin Wang dropped the nail to the floor.

Bonner writhed and turned white, moaning through set lips. Lin Wang ripped out another fingernail. Bonner screamed.

"Will you sign that confession?" said Lin Wang.

"No!" roared Bonner.

The pliers came down slowly this time. Bonner flinched. Lin Wang smiled and jerked back. Once more the pliers descended.

"I'll sign!" cried Bonner.

They unfastened his right hand and slid a board under his arm. They thrust a pen between his shaking fingers. From his left hand blood dripped slowly to the floor.

Bonner wrote what Lin Wang dictated.

> I, George Bonner, do hereby confess to the murder of Captain Randolph for the purposes of robbery aboard the SS *Rangoon* off the Coast of China. I murdered Captain Randolph with a belaying pin, crushing his skull, found the combination to the safe among his papers and extracted the loot. On request, the money and certificates are waiting at the shop of Loi Chung—Nanking Road.
>
> Signed: George Bonner
> Witness: Yang Ch'ieu

The pliers came down slowly this time. Bonner flinched.
Lin Wang smiled and jerked back. . . .
"I'll sign!" cried Bonner.

Lin Wang read the paper over, watched by Bonner's pain-deadened eyes.

"You did kill him, didn't you?" said Lin Wang, affably.

Bonner gave him a sick nod.

Lin Wang reached into his desk and extracted a German automatic pistol. "Any prayers, my good Bonner?"

"Jesus! You're not going to—"

The concussion of the shot boomed through the small room. Blue smoke eddied about Bonner's chair. Lin Wang fired again. Bonner slumped, a bullet between his eyes.

"Take him out," said Lin Wang with an airy wave of his dangling hand. He blew the smoke out of the muzzle and placed the automatic back in his desk.

"This confession," said Lin Wang, "is valid and perfectly satisfactory to authorities. Had I turned you over to them, they might have cleared you and that would have been that. But now, Kurt Reid . . . "

"What's your game?" demanded Kurt.

"Game? That suggests hunting, doesn't it? Then, Kurt Reid you are going hunting."

"You're insane!"

"Of course," said Lin Wang. "I find it most pleasant. You are supposed to be a fighter and you can get by where a Chinese could not. This confession I keep here with me, in my jacket. When you have killed your game, bring back its scalp and you shall have the confession."

"You mean I've got to buy that with murder?"

"Precisely, Kurt Reid. You are a very intelligent gentleman, I must say. I shall make very sure that you do not escape. In fact, I shall lend you Captain Yang Ch'ieu and six members of the Death Squad.

"I choose you because you may escape unscathed in the Japanese lines. Yes, the Japanese lines. You are to proceed to Kalgan on the Great Wall, there find one they call *Takeki*, the Courageous, a notorious spy, very harmful to the peace of China, one who is responsible for much of this Autonomy move. You will kill this *Takeki*, and when you have brought me evidence that you have done so, you shall have this confession. Then you will be a free man.

"But if you do not kill this *Takeki*, through Captain Yang I will inform the authorities where you may be apprehended and I shall have men appear at your trial as witnesses against you, thereby making it certain that you die a criminal. There is no escape for you.

"And if you go too wrong in this, you saw what happened to this man Bonner. Perhaps I would not trust the authorities. But however that may be, Kurt Reid, kill *Takeki* and you are a free man."

"So that's why you did all this."

"Of course. But do not make the mistake of thinking that this *Takeki* is anything less than a demon. He may try you very much before you finish with him. My own men could not approach him at all, but you, as a white man, speaking their language, should be able to do it and escape.

"I might remind you, Kurt Reid, that something of the fate of China rests on your shoulders."

"You went far enough around to put it there," snapped Kurt. "All right. I'll try it. Let me up from here."

Captain Yang unlashed him and pulled him to his feet. Although Kurt was tall, Captain Yang loomed over him like a mountain which has a summer house at its summit.

Captain Yang said, "I think we will have a very enjoyable trip, bucko mate."

CHAPTER FOUR

Danger in Kalgan

IT was a very different looking Kurt Reid who arrived one night on the Peking-Suiyuan Railway in Kalgan. He stepped from the train in the company of a gigantic merchant who had six servants unload their baggage.

Kurt Reid was dressed in a well-tailored dark suit and wore a pearl gray hat. He was clean shaved again and looked as much unlike the bucko mate as had the prisoner of Lin Wang. His clear black eyes searched through the crowd as do those of men about to hang, and he found no friendship or promise of rescue. Yang Ch'ieu nudged him, as a signal to move along.

They picked their way through littered streets toward a small hotel. Japanese soldiers were in evidence everywhere, dressed in mustard-colored uniforms, officers marked by red cap bands. Guards with fixed bayonets stood before many entrances. Japan was about to take over North China, and Kalgan, near the Great Wall, was the jumping off place.

Kurt Reid felt very tired and down in the mouth. He had been unable to locate Anne Carsten in Shanghai, although he had tried his best to find her at the risk of his own liberty. And he had approached the puzzle of Lin Wang's move no further.

On the surface, it would appear that Lin Wang was fighting

33

to retain North China, and to do so, Lin Wang considered it vital that this *Takeki* person, supposed to be a Japanese spy, be killed. But the closer Kurt Reid came to it, the more convinced he was that killing a Japanese spy in the Japanese lines was an impossibility.

But with that confession of Bonner's as a lure and with Yang here beside him, Kurt knew he would try.

As they rounded a corner and pressed their way through a camel caravan which had stopped in the street, Kurt drew a sudden breath of surprise, causing Yang to look down at him quickly.

Kurt walked on calmly enough although he was certain that he had seen a familiar face in the crowd. Maybe all White Russians looked alike, and maybe there was more than one fur hat and coat like that in China, but something more than sight had given him his information.

Varinka Savischna was here! He had seen her entering a shop.

That bothered him more than a little, and heartened him a great deal. On one hand he hated to see Varinka in a Japanese town, but on the other, her presence might be an omen of good luck. If he could see her, maybe he would be able to find out where this *Takeki* might be found.

With springier stride he followed Yang into the hotel and registered. The six servants, hiding their warlike faces under their hats, made their way back to the lesser ground floor quarters.

Kurt's room was a small affair, boasting only a bed and a

chair and a picture of the Mikado, put up by the hotel keeper, doubtless, to show Japan that he had their cause at heart.

Yang had gone to his own room, and for a moment Kurt fondled the idea of getting out and away. But when he looked down into the street he saw one of the six slowly puffing a cigarette at the hotel entrance. The man was armed, and even though a street fight might give away their identity, these guards knew what to expect from Lin Wang as the price of failure.

A man in a blue gown thrust his head into the doorway and said, "Everything all right, sir?"

"Yes," said Kurt. "Quite all right."

But the small yellow-faced man did not go away. He entered and patted the bedspread smooth and adjusted the pillow. "Anything I might tell the gentleman?" he said.

"No," replied Kurt.

"Pardoning your honor, but this one is a good guide. He knows all things."

Kurt studied the man for a moment and then said, "You can tell me something, if you promise to forget the question immediately. Where can I find this one known as *Takeki*?"

The other shook his head. "I do not know." He went out.

Kurt stretched himself on the bed and thought for a long time. He wondered how he was going to find this Japanese spy in the first place. Perhaps the spy would come to see him. That was a plan. If Kurt let it be known that he had some vital information about South China, the spy might present himself. Distasteful as the job was, it had to be done.

He wondered for a long time why Varinka was here, and how he could find her again. But then Kalgan was not so big and Varinka's exotic beauty was easily spotted in an Oriental crowd. Odd that he had crossed her track again.

His ponderings were interrupted by a knock on the door. Without knowing quite why he did so, Kurt glanced out of the window and saw that the guard was gone.

He opened the door and fell back. A Japanese officer and a squad of infantrymen blocked the passage. Their dark faces were set in a military glower and their caps sat precisely upon the tops of their heads. Their blued bayonets shimmered dully.

The officer said, "You are under arrest. Quietly come with us."

No man is fool enough to launch himself against eight bayonets. Kurt picked up his hat, set it on the back of his head and fell in between the files.

Yang burst out of his room and stood gaping at the squad. Then, startling in his iron face, two great tears welled up out of his eyes and ran down his cheeks. Yang was an excellent actor.

Yang fell upon Kurt and wept loudly. "Do not take him, *taichō*. He is my friend!" wailed Yang, shaking like a mountain in an earthquake. But under cover of the sobs he whispered in a voice like a saw, "Keep your mouth shut, fool. Killing will be too good for you."

The captain pried Yang away and pushed him back against the wall. Yang submitted tearfully, and Kurt was led away.

The squad marched him through the crowded street. People paused to stare and point. Little children, faces round and mouths filled with jeers, ran on either side of the files.

"It is some great traitor," ran the whisper. "They are going to execute him!"

Kurt watched the cloth shoes going up and down on either side of him. He was unable to account for this sudden turn of events and he looked bleakly ahead to even a worse fate than that promised by Yang.

They went into a big stone house which served as Japanese headquarters and Kurt was left standing before a rough desk. The man who sat there was small and wiry. His eyes were hidden behind plate-glass spectacles which made him look like a submarine monster. His hair stood straight up, like a pig-bristle brush.

Kurt saw another beside the desk, a small man in a blue gown. The man he had taken for a bellhop at the hotel.

"Is this the man?" said the officer at the desk.

"Yes, sir. He asked me about *Takeki,* sir."

The officer nodded and peered nearsightedly at Kurt. "Why did you ask that question? What is your name?"

"My name is Smith," said Kurt. "I was merely curious, that is all."

"Please do not lie to me," said the officer, rubbing his hands thoughtfully together. "Your name is Kurt Reid. Now go on."

Kurt blinked. It seemed that he was fated to be known mysteriously by everyone. How had this information come to this Japanese headquarters?

"Why, yes, so it is," said Kurt. "But I was still curious about *Takeki.* I have some information for him."

"For him? Ah, well, you can give it to me."

"Only to *Takeki.*"

"You're obstinate," said the Japanese. "Ah, well, *taichō,* take this man back to the cells." And to Kurt, "If *Takeki* comes, perhaps you will be able to give your information first hand. If not . . ." The officer shrugged and went back to work. Kurt fell into the files again and was presently thrust into a barred enclosure which resembled a jail less than a wild animal cage. He was the only prisoner there.

The door clanged and Kurt was again left to his thoughts. At first he was very angry. He stomped up and down the paved floor, swearing and kicking at the bars, but at last his anger burned itself out and he sat down on a bench.

"One jail after another," said Kurt. "I should have let them hang me the first time."

He grinned at that and stretched out, glad to have a few hours' sleep away from the scrutiny of Yang and the six members of the Death Squad.

After what seemed a minute or two, but which was really six hours, Kurt was awakened by the slither of a rope into the enclosure.

He propped himself up on one elbow and stared about him, rubbing the sleep from his eyes. He was cold, and the bench had bitten deeply into his hard body, but he had the feeling that something was wrong and he came alert in an instant.

He saw stars over him and noticed for the first time that the enclosure had no roof. The bars were bent into hooks at the top to discourage anyone from climbing out. Next he saw a long snakelike thing which made him jump.

He touched it in the darkness and found that it was a rope. Puzzled and holding his breath, he stood up.

A scraping sound came from the top of the bars, and presently Kurt saw a man outlined against the sky. Slowly the man began to descend.

Until it was too late, Kurt thought that Varinka had located him and was about to engineer his escape. He stood by until the hazily seen Chinese was firmly on the floor.

A knife glittered in the stranger's hand. The Chinese took a step toward Kurt.

"Captain Yang," said the guard in a low voice, "has passed the sentence upon you. You have failed Lin Wang, you are no further use to him. I am a member of the Death Squad."

The man dived in and the knife came down. Kurt was rocked back. The bars creaked as they were struck. Kurt caught the knife wrist and pried it back. He had been too startled to cry out, and now he needed all his breath.

The garlic-reeking mouth of the Chinese was close to Kurt's face. The man was trying to bring up his knees for a numbing blow. Kurt drove in his right fist and heard it crunch against a bone.

The Chinese gave ground slowly. Kurt pushed up with all his might, striving to keep back the knife, but he was dealing with a man who had fought with steel his whole life.

The arm went limp. Kurt was thrown off his balance. He let go the wrist for a fraction of a second. The knife came down with vicious strength.

Kurt lurched back, deflecting the blade by making it hit

his shoulder broadside. He doubled up and dropped to the floor. The Chinese attempted to pin Kurt down, but Kurt suddenly exploded.

On top of the Chinese, Kurt secured the dagger hand with his knee and then with both hands, Kurt raised the close-shaven head and slammed it back to the concrete. Once, twice, the third time the head did not bounce. The man's eyes rolled far up into his head. A sticky smear of blood stained the concrete black in the starlight.

Kurt stood up and rubbed his sleeve across his forehead. He felt drained and shaking. One slip and he would be lying there instead of the Chinese.

Abruptly he remembered that other members of the Death Squad might be waiting outside.

"Guard!" cried Kurt. *"Mamori!"*

The rope had looked inviting until he thought about Yang. Now a barred enclosure was just the thing.

Doors slammed, men came running, rifles clanking. Flashlights stabbed through the bars.

Japanese entered and looked down at the Chinese and then at Kurt.

"He tried to kill me," began Kurt.

"But how did he get in?" demanded an officer.

Kurt pointed to the rope.

"Who was he?"

Kurt thought it best to be discreet on that point. "A man who thought I had wronged him."

"That's likely," said the officer with a grunt. "He would hate very well to make an attempt on your life in here."

The men started to go away, taking the dead man with them. "Wait a minute," said Kurt. "I'm not going to stay in here."

"Why not?"

"The man might have friends."

"All right," said the officer, "come into the guard room, the *tsumesho.*"

That suited Kurt very well, and he was escorted out of the enclosure and ordered to sit down along the wall beside a small heater. The soldiers there looked curiously at him.

When the officer had gone, a small fellow with a pale face and a scholarly air said politely, "How do you do," in English. It was probably all that he knew.

In Japanese, the others began to talk about Kurt and wonder why he was there. Their conversation continued for a half hour and was of a very personal and critical nature. They discussed how pale Kurt was and how big, and said that he must be a very great thief because all foreign devils were great thieves.

Kurt listened to them with a blank face for a while. Their inquisitiveness made him forget Varinka and Anne Carsten and Lin Wang. He began to cheer up.

In Japanese, Kurt said, "Would you mind getting me a glass of water, *tomodachi*?"

The scholarly little man leaped up in surprise and scurried to the skin bag which hung in the corner. He came back with the drink.

"Thank you," said Kurt, drinking. "Tell me, *tomodachi*, is it a crime here in Kalgan to speak of *Takeki*?"

The scholarly one shook his head. "No, but it is dangerous. *Takeki* is one we call the Courageous. I cannot say any more. Is that why you are here?"

"I merely wanted to see *Takeki*. I had some information for him."

"For him?" said the soldiers all together.

The officer had said that. Kurt thought it queer. He decided not to talk about *Takeki*.

A larger Japanese, with rugged features, almost Western, said in a complimentary tone, "That was a good job you did on that Chinese one. He looked very strong. Why did he go in there to attack you?"

"He didn't like me," said Kurt.

"All these Chinese are fools," said the scholarly one. "For a long time we left them alone and did nothing to them. For centuries. They tried to take our country from us twice, and now when we merely want to police theirs and wipe out some of their so-called warlords such as Lin Wang, the whole world cries against it. It is very strange. I cannot understand it at all."

"They think you are trying to capture China," said Kurt.

"No, that isn't what they think," said the big one. "They are afraid of us. It would be a good thing if someone took over China and made a nation out of it and cut down this killing and made the people behave. All Chinese are fools. The world is afraid that Japan will grow powerful if Japan has China's manpower. Perhaps it will. Can you blame Japan for trying?"

Kurt nodded. He could see the Japanese side of things and

he had no particular political views. Japan and China were farthest from his worries at that minute.

He was thinking furiously about that confession. He would have to get it somehow. He couldn't run away from the law the rest of his life. Maybe if he explained to Yang . . .

A door swung open and a voice said, "Foreigner, *Takeki* is waiting to speak with you."

Kurt got to his feet. He was about to face the man he had been sent to kill. He wondered what he would say to the Japanese.

He walked slowly out into the other room and stared across the desks.

"There is *Takeki,* foreigner," said the officer again.

Kurt swallowed hard.

He was staring at Varinka Savischna.

CHAPTER FIVE

The Japanese Spy

IT took a moment or two for Kurt Reid to recover from his surprise, but his silence was unnoticed. Varinka Savischna came forward, holding out her hands to him, smiling.

"My dear Kurt," said Varinka. "I am surprised, but very glad to see you. I hope these compatriots of mine did not cause you any inconvenience."

She was taller than the Japanese, and she carried herself with a conscious pride of beauty. Her beautiful broad face was smiling.

Kurt took her hands. He could do nothing else. "I did not know that you—"

"And what news do you bring me from the south?" she said, interrupting him.

Kurt glanced at the Japanese. They eyed him with a suspicion of hostility. "Nothing of any moment, Varinka."

"But certainly you must have *something*, to come so far to find me."

"Oh, yes, perhaps you'd be interested to know that . . . that Lin Wang . . . But then I would feel better if I could impart this information to you privately."

"Of course. I have a car outside and I am living a short distance away. You are probably hungry and you must come with me to get something to eat. We can talk then."

45

Kurt felt the leaden silence of the room. He felt very uncomfortable. He could feel the thoughts of the Japanese. They were not at all sure of him, those fellows, and he knew they were telling themselves that they would keep their eye on him. He felt a chill run up and down his spine when a soldier clattered his rifle against the wall. The brown eyes stabbed him. Death and danger were heavy in the room.

Varinka did not seem to notice it. Her fur-topped boots whispered over the hard floor as she led Kurt out to the waiting car. Three sentries, carrying their rifles in their hands, swung on to the running board. Kurt felt that he was under arrest.

A cold wind was sweeping across the dead brown hills, stirring up dust through the blackness. Kalgan was silent and without lights. It slept uneasily under the heel of its conqueror from across the Yellow Sea.

They arrived at a small enclosure and went through a wide gate, which was quickly clanged shut behind them. The sound had a finality to it which Kurt did not like.

The guards dropped to the cobblestones of the courtyard. Kurt looked about to see that this house, like most Chinese houses, was built in three separate huts, each one serving a different purpose. The gray stone walls reminded him of a prison.

But the furnishings of the room into which he was led belied the exterior. Fine silks were draped along the walls. Colorful cushions were strewn about the border of a tan and black carpet. A fire was crackling cheerfully in the fireplace. The heavy odor of Russian incense, far too sweet, caught in Kurt's throat.

Varinka threw off her coat and tossed the cap aside. She

sat down on a cushion and placed her left hand on the floor for support. She smiled at Kurt.

The three guards were outside somewhere, walking back and forth, feet resonant upon the stones.

A black-gowned amah came in, bowed, saw that Varinka had a guest and quickly went away. She returned in a moment with excellent whisky and a tray of food, which she placed on a chow bench.

Kurt ate slowly, watching Varinka, and listening to the footsteps of the guard. Finally he said, "This is rotten business."

Varinka shrugged. "One has to live."

"You mean you're a spy for these yellow devils? You mean you're willing to help them take over China. Not that I care what happens to China, but after all the Japanese . . ."

"One has to live," said Varinka.

"But to be guarded like this—"

"Those guards are there because the Japanese are suspicious of you, Kurt. You have no official status here." She paused as though unwilling to say more. Then, with a glance up at the small window, she leaned closer to him and lowered her voice, "I'm afraid they think that I . . . A spy can never tell who his friends and enemies are."

He caught a glimpse of fear in her eyes when she said that, but the expression was instantly gone.

"Tell me what happened to you," she said, lighting a long cigarette.

Kurt snorted. "They picked me up after you left the house. Lin Wang's men, I mean. Lin Wang has a confession waiting for me in Shanghai and if—"

47

The food gagged him suddenly. He realized then that this *Takeki* and Varinka were one and the same person. He had been sent to Kalgan to kill Varinka, and if he did not kill her, his own life was forfeit. But then, hadn't one of Yang's men tried to kill him? Wasn't that bond absolved? But still, the confession was in the hands of Lin Wang, and Lin Wang had ordered this thing to be done.

"What's the matter?" said Varinka suddenly. "You're white as a ghost!" She moved closer to him. "Are you ill?"

"No . . . no, no."

"Then go on. Tell me."

Kurt hid his face behind a large drink of the whisky. You can't tell a person that you have been sent to kill them.

"He sent me North, told me to leave China," said Kurt.

She did not believe him, but neither did she question him. She merely said, "Funny thing for Lin Wang to do. He usually uses his Death Squad."

"But I was glad you got away," said Kurt, feeling very uneasy.

"Never worry about me," replied Varinka. "There's a panel and a secret staircase, and another door in that house, in the native city."

"I still can't figure out about my escape, though."

Varinka laughed at him and hugged her knees. "I knew that you were to be let loose from the *Rangoon*, and so I placed a sampan near the ship so that you wouldn't have to swim ashore. You must have evaded the men Lin Wang sent to follow you, but my man picked you up and trailed you to the tea house. I waited there for you and my messenger. I needed a good, strong man I could trust, and I knew that Lin Wang

48

wanted you for some purpose or other. I was going to steal
his man from him."

"What did you want me for?"

"I don't trust Chinese, much less Japanese. I thought you
would be able to help me and I knew I could help you. I had
an idea that I could prove you innocent, and you had such a
reputation as a fighter and as a linguist, I thought it a shame
to let such material run around loose. And maybe . . . maybe,
I was just being kind. I don't know. It amused me.

"Tell me, Kurt, did you see Anne Carsten there?"

"Why, yes, of course," and for some reason he could not
define he felt himself crimson.

"Ah, so you did meet her, eh? A fine woman, isn't she? So
young to be living alone in the native city. She must have
taken quite a fancy to you, from the way you look. She is
always taken with sailors."

"Wait a minute," said Kurt. "I think she's a swell kid."

Varinka laughed delightedly. "Then you love her, eh?"

"No, of course not."

"Why 'of course not' so very gruff? Would that be
impossible? Tell me, Kurt, if you were to choose between us,
which one would you take?"

He crimsoned again. "An unfair question."

"Oh, but never mind. Anne Carsten has such a hard time
of it. You know her father died in Shanghai six months ago.
Did you know that? It was said that the Death Squad had
some little thing to do with it. Carsten was far too interested
in Chinese politics."

"The poor kid," said Kurt. "What happened?"

"Why, her father was a merchant prince, and he thought Lin Wang shouldn't have so much responsibility. He died for it, that's all. Lin Wang is a devil."

Kurt agreed with her there. Once again he saw the horrible nightmare of the man's scaly face, the dirt-grimed wrinkles, the limply hanging and clattering hands, the hunched back. But the mention of Lin Wang brought something else to him. Lin Wang held liberty in his shaking hands. Lin Wang had sent Kurt Reid to Kalgan to kill one named *Takeki* the Courageous, who was also known as Varinka Savischna.

"You are very thoughtful," said Varinka. "What is wrong?"

If the Japanese guessed his mission there, Kurt knew that sudden death would be the mildest of fates.

Suddenly a gunshot roared outside, blasting through the night. Feet clattered over the cobblestones. Shrill Japanese voices cried out.

In one motion, Kurt swept Varinka back against the wall and knocked over the lamp, bringing darkness to the room. Varinka gasped. Kurt felt her under his hand, and the treacherous thought that he could kill her easily now made him shudder.

The glass crashed from the window and something thumped into the room. Another shot roared and then the guards came back swearing. Cautiously Kurt fumbled about on the floor and discovered something which felt like a grenade. He picked it up as though it was hot, about ready to explode. Then he realized that it was a stone with a paper tied around it. He knelt against the wall and undid the sheet.

The fireplace flickered up for a moment, throwing Kurt's

shadow hugely against the silken drapes. Varinka crawled toward him.

In that sudden splash of light, Kurt made out the note. It was in English and it said:

We are waiting. Death there will cancel death here.

Kurt crumpled up the note in his hand. Varinka's fingers tried to reach it, fingers which were suddenly strong. Kurt jerked the note away and threw it wildly toward the fireplace.

The guards were coming in through the door.

"What is wrong?" bawled a Japanese.

Varinka stood up and ordered Kurt to his feet. The other two guards came in, panting. They had been running.

"What did you find outside?" said Varinka.

The guard shook his head. "Nothing. Men climbed up on a roof across the street and threw something toward your window. Did anything land in here? They got away."

Varinka picked up the stone and looked at it. The twine which had held the note was still there. She looked long at Kurt.

Taking in the situation, one of the guards looked about in front of the fireplace. He found the note lying a foot away from the flames. He spread it out on the hearth, kneeling there, rifle on the floor beside him.

"I cannot read it," he said. "It is in English."

Varinka looked down at it and was about to pick it up. An officer came from nowhere and pushed her aside. He sent a thin scornful glance at Varinka and took the note.

"I can read it," said the officer. He scanned the letters for a moment and then read them aloud.

For a full minute the room was silent, and then Varinka spun on Kurt, her fists clenched. "I understand now, you beast. I understand. You were sent here by Lin Wang to murder me. You want to kill me! And outside Captain Yang is waiting for you to see that you do the job. And if you fail he will murder you!"

The officer gained in height. He slowly pulled his automatic from its holster and slid off the safety catch. His wiry hair bristled out from under his cap like an angry dog's.

"No," said Varinka, bitterly. "We need not stain our hands with such as he. Captain Yang is waiting, Mr. Reid. He will be disappointed if you are late."

Kurt looked at the door and the square of blackness it embraced. He started to move away. But Varinka would not so easily let him go. She was upon him in an instant. She struck him with her right hand and then thrust him away from her.

"You filthy beast! Get out! Get out!"

Kurt turned on his heel, amazed, and went through the door. The Japanese officer laughed behind him. The guards raised their rifles hopefully.

Kurt went on across the yard toward the gate. Captain Yang was waiting. Captain Yang had tried to kill him once, and now . . .

He started through the entrance, staring bleakly at the dark, deserted street. From any corner death might strike.

Not until then did he notice that his jacket pocket was sagging. He put his hand inside and encountered an automatic pistol. Astounded, he fingered it, turning it over before his face. Suddenly he understood. He looked back toward the hut.

Varinka Savischna had put that there. She had not sent him away unarmed. She had made him go because no chance was left at Japanese hands.

He knew, standing there, already expecting the numbing shots of bullets through his back, that Varinka loved him and that he loved her.

CHAPTER SIX

Any Man's Prey

K ALGAN, at the hour of two AM, had the appearance of a tomb. The darkness, in spite of the brisk wind which came down from the mountains, had a clammy, dismal air, like waiting death.

The houses, square against the lighter sky, stood out in regimental rows. The walls which hid private gardens from the public eye were black scowls along the street.

Kurt had the feeling, and rightly, that he was being watched. He went slowly, following the deepest shadows. The convict under the executioner's knife knew that death was coming, and from whence it would come, and at what instant—but Kurt did not know. He could only guess, and wait for the stab of thunder and sparks around the next wall. He did not think he would ever hear the shot or feel the impact of the bullet.

Captain Yang, in a rage against Lin Wang and Kurt, unable to carry out the duty assigned to him, not quite sure just who this *Takeki* might be, would deal a death of vengeance. The mountain of flesh undoubtedly felt that Kurt was to blame for everything that had happened here in Kalgan. One of Lin Wang's men was already dead, his body in the possession of the Japanese. Yang had given Kurt one last chance and, in Yang's eyes, Kurt had failed.

Kurt had a feeling of fatalistic helplessness. The gods of China were against him and he could do nothing to extricate himself. Perhaps he would be able to fight his way out, but knowing that the Japanese would get him if Yang did not, anything he did was futile.

He could only walk close to the wall, silently waiting, and watch for the powder flame which would mark his finish.

He thought about Varinka for a while. She was a brave kid and she might have incurred the wrath of the Japanese when she gave him a chance at freedom. Sooner or later, if Kurt managed to stay alive throughout the night, the suspicious men would come to the conclusion that she was not being above-board with them. Perhaps even now her power was slipping. He had noticed but little courtesy displayed toward her. The guards were not so much guarding her life as guarding her.

Kurt stopped then, brought up sweating with a terrible knowledge. If he lived out the night, then the Japanese would think that he had gone free with information destined for the enemy. They could not help but think that.

But if he was found cold and dead in the filth of the street, then Varinka might have a chance.

His sense of humor came to his rescue then. He laughed silently, harshly, leaning back against the gray wall. He had thought earlier that his own safety depended upon Varinka's death. And now Varinka's life depended upon his own demise. Fate had spun the tables.

Anne Carsten would think . . . He paused then, and wondered what she would think. He hadn't meant anything to her, but Anne Carsten recurred constantly in his thoughts. She was beautiful, even more so than Varinka. Of all the women Kurt had known, those two seemed to him the finest, the most desirable. Perhaps he did think a great deal of Varinka, perhaps he even loved her, but it was unthinkable to marry a White Russian woman in China.

He laughed again, feeling light-headed, his thoughts very clear. Here he was worrying about Anne Carsten and Varinka when he would not live another hour.

What he wouldn't give for a shot at Lin Wang now. The twisted, scaly leper had taken Kurt in, right enough. But Lin Wang had not been smart. He could not have known that Kurt knew the one called *Takeki*. Lin Wang had not suspected that a man would stay his killing hand for the sake of gallantry, even when the killer's life itself was at stake. Lin Wang, in his warped cruelty, did not know many things.

For a moment Kurt wondered at his own stupidity. Things were clear enough to him now. He was going to die. An electric light bulb, before it burns out, flares into sudden, final brilliance.

The reason, Kurt knew, for Lin Wang's sending him here to Kalgan to kill *Takeki* was sound enough. Funny Kurt hadn't thought about it before. Of course. Yang had his orders. When *Takeki* was dead, Yang would turn *Takeki*'s killer over to the Japanese, at no risk to himself. That would simplify matters for Lin Wang. *Takeki*'s murderer would not be looked for in China. The Japanese, all too often, had demanded huge indemnities for the killing of one of their people—and Varinka was certainly that.

57

And now that Kurt had refused, Yang would kill him, having no further use for him. Again Kurt laughed. He had been a fool. The confession had meant nothing. Kurt would not have lived anyway.

Pausing there in the shadow of the wall saved his life.

From the next corner came the whisper of slippers on the paving stones.

The Death Squad had tired of waiting.

Kurt saw a black blot detach itself from the building ahead and start down toward him, groping along. Something shiny glittered in the outstretched hand.

The man came slowly, a step at a time, undecided as to Kurt's position. Kurt sank deeper into the shadow.

The Chinese came on, an inch at a time. A shaft of light from a high window struck the untroubled face. The Chinese came placidly enough, unworried by his mission. Killing had become second nature to the Death Squad.

Kurt drew out the automatic and determined to make a stand. Where were the others? Was this one alone? Did Kurt dare risk a shot?

The ominous silence of Kalgan blanketed the street. The wind moaned a little around a corner. The sound of Kurt's automatic slide sounded like a sledgehammer blow.

The Chinese stopped, listening, probing the shadows with narrow, killer's eyes.

Kurt raised the pistol, extended it to full arm's length. The shadow covered the groove down the slide. Carefully Kurt compressed his whole hand. Odd how steady he was. He knew that he could not miss.

The sound of Kurt's automatic slide
sounded like a sledgehammer blow.
The Chinese stopped, listening, probing
the shadows with narrow, killer's eyes.

Flame and sparks ribboned like a lightning flash. The Chinese cried out, threw up his hands and stumbled forward. His arms were down again, clutching his chest. His own gun clattered to the paving. He tripped and sprawled, spread-eagled.

A shout came from the corner. Two men leaped into sight and came running. Kurt started to race away, and then knew that he would make too good a target out of his shadow.

Kurt spun about and leaped up to the top of the wall. Broken glass had been set up in the cement to discourage robbers. Kurt's hands were gashed into a slippery mess.

But he had no thought of pain. He swung over. A gun roared below him as he crouched for an instant at the top, silhouetted against the sky.

He dropped to the garden and whipped his way through a line of shrubs against the wall. Water shimmered in front of him. He skirted it, tripped on a loose stone, and for a moment pushed himself along across gravel on his hands and knees.

The Death Squad had found the postern. Already they were hammering against it with their brawny shoulders. Kurt's one thought was to get across the garden and over the other wall.

He heard wood splinter and knew that the postern gate had given way. He scrambled through a flower bed and stepped through another pool. Before him, dimly seen, a one-legged iron stork gazed wisely at him. At his right a metal turtle seemed to bob up and down. But it was only the water lapping.

Kurt reached the other wall. Feet were grinding the

gravel paths in rapid pursuit. With only one thought—to get away—Kurt tried to scale the wall.

He looked up then and his heart dropped within him. This was no wall at all, but the side of a house. There was no getting away.

Men floundered through a pool and came on. Kurt turned to face them.

The Chinese loomed hugely against the lighter gray of the far wall. But they did not seem to have faces or hands, only arms. They were great shadows come to life without wits, with only the will to slaughter. They knew that they had to be fast. The Japanese guard would be coming soon to locate the firing.

With his back pushed against the chill stone, Kurt raised the automatic and fired.

A shadow in the lead went down and stumbled back to splash into the pool beside the iron stork.

Kurt moved hastily to one side. An answering shot whined away from the stone beside his head.

Crouching low, steadying his gun on his arm, Kurt drew a bead on another Chinese to the left. The man and his two mates faltered. That was all Kurt wanted. While he was in the dark, the others were in relief, whether they knew it or not, against the lighter gray wall.

Kurt's target leaped sideways, crying out and stumbling. His two mates changed their position hastily and started to close in toward the man they could but dimly see.

Rock chips flew beside Kurt's arm. He shifted his position.

One of the Chinese was almost on him. Kurt leaped out, straight into the fellow's face. Kurt jammed the muzzle catch deep into the yielding stomach and pulled the trigger. The shot sounded dead.

A blast of pain went through Kurt's shoulder. He whipped away, carrying a knife with him, embedded in his flesh. With a roar the last Chinese flung himself upon Lin Wang's victim.

They went down into shrubbery with a crash, the Chinese on top. Kurt, anger setting red balls dancing before his face, felt that he embraced a clawing tiger. Kurt kicked hard with both feet. Fingers were locating his throat. Kurt's gun was gone.

He realized dimly that something was white hot in his shoulder. The man's knife.

Kurt rolled to one side, struggling. The fingers sank deep into his windpipe. The stars above him began to spin crazily. His chest was burning for lack of air.

He reached across the Chinese's arms, toward his own shoulder, trying to think, forcing himself to do the thing. With a tremendous effort, Kurt clutched the knife hilt and tugged the weapon free from his own flesh.

He twisted again, trying to get arm room. He held the knife high above the other's back and brought it down. He pulled it out and brought it down a second time. The blade would not move.

The world was black for seconds, and then the fingers eased up. Throat rattling, the Chinese slumped down on the man he had almost killed.

For seconds Kurt lay dragging in precious air. He had never before known how good it was to just breathe. But after a little he assembled his strength and thrust the body away from him. The Chinese was like an overweight tree, already rigid.

Kurt got to his feet and fumbled about for his gun. He could not find the one he had been given. In its place he took a Colt .45 which had fallen from the hand of the second man he had killed.

He went through the garden toward the shattered gate, stopped beside each body, looking for Yang.

But Yang was not there. Yang was still alive, still waiting for the kill.

From the street came the sound of running men. Equipment clanked. The Japanese guards were on their way to determine the reason for the shooting. Kurt knew that death waited for him at their hands.

He ran down the wall and found another gate. Shouts echoed through the garden. Kurt fumbled with the lock and finally opened it. He slipped out into an alley and quietly eased down its length to another street.

From the direction of the garden came the shouts of the guards. Soon all Kalgan would be searched. Kurt wondered if they would realize who had fought there, and why. But whoever had, would find the going hard before a Japanese court.

Kurt was still mad. He did not give his sliced hands and his gouged shoulder a thought. He felt that he could whip the whole Japanese army with a pop gun and that if he met Lin Wang in the midst of all his guards, it would be an easy matter to blow the man down.

For a long while the bucko mate had been tossed about by worry and by cross purposes. But now he was mad. He didn't care what happened to him. He was walking out to even up the score, and if he kept going like he started, nothing short of beheading would stop him.

He took the middle of the street with a swagger. His face, usually so handsome, was twisted up into a hard-boiled scowl. His gait was a sea roll and he carried the automatic in plain sight. He was insane and he knew it and didn't care.

The bucko mate, hero of many a barroom brawl and sea fight, was stepping into his own: fast action.

He headed straight for Varinka's house. To hell with the guards! Varinka was in danger. He knew it without thinking. He couldn't let her down. Without that automatic he would have been an easy victim for the Death Squad.

He came to her gate, threw back the iron and stepped arrogantly through, ready to blast down the first foe he saw, bayonets notwithstanding.

It came to him as a shock that the courtyard was deserted. He walked straight toward the hut, expecting a challenge which refused to come. He stopped irresolutely before the door, staring about him.

Something had happened here. Something was wrong.

He kicked in the panel and stepped into the room. The fireplace had burned down to a pulsating red pile of coals. The shadows of the room were deep. The lamp was still overturned, spilling bean oil across the Oriental black and tan carpet.

The sound of a sob came to Kurt. Instantly he felt better. Maybe Varinka was still here. Perhaps . . .

Something moved in the corner. He strode toward it and beheld Varinka's amah huddled behind a drapery. Disgusted, he hauled her forth and in a machine-gun tattoo of Chinese, demanded news of the Russian girl.

"They take her away. They arrest her. I know nothing."

Varinka arrested? Then he was right. His own release was likely to cause her death. The Japanese did not question a victim for long. The Japanese were more likely to hold the trial after the firing squad.

Varinka was arrested and Kurt knew that she would die. For a moment he felt a helpless nausea and then, hefting the Colt .45, he went out into the courtyard and walked swiftly toward the Japanese headquarters. . . .

CHAPTER SEVEN

Sentenced to Death

THE building did not shed a great deal of light. It clutched shadows to its cold walls and gave off a feeling of menace. Two windows sprayed yellow jets into the street. Kurt heard the wind moan past a cornice.

Japanese voices came from within, purring, assured voices. Outside a car stood, its driver slumped wearily over the wheel. Behind the car was a truck, but no one was in the cab.

Kurt came as close as possible to the window. By standing on a loose paving block he could see in without being seen himself.

Varinka stood before a group of men, who sat indolently in chairs. Their caps and red bands showed that they were officers and their faces displayed a merciless arrogance which was heightened by the effect of their black, bristly hair. Two of them puffed on cigarettes which they held before their sharp faces with nicotine-stained fingers. Guards with fixed bayonets were posted about the room.

They were questioning Varinka in Japanese and their tone was ugly, showing that her guilt was a foregone conclusion. But they were not trying her for the thing Kurt thought.

Varinka's broad face was without fear. Her slightly slanted eyes were scornful. Her high cheekbones were stained with the crimson of anger. She looked regal—a lioness pulled down by jackals.

"What you say is not true," said Varinka.

A small, bony officer giggled. "*Takeki* would go well in a *Nō* drama, *sayō?*"

A bitter-faced fellow with eyes as black as the pit, obviously the ranking *yakunin*, probably a *taishō*, silenced the bony one with a scowl.

"You have lied out of this two times, *Takeki*. You told us that this was some sort of intrigue you were planning. The officers believed you—I did not. They see now that I should have been more determined in my condemnation."

"Bah," said Varinka, coldly, "you hate me, *taishō*, because I would have nothing to do with you and with none of your officers. You hate me, all of you, because I had too much power."

The *taishō* smiled cruelly. "This time you cannot escape. This afternoon I received a letter from Shanghai. Some of the things you reported to us were lies, and you know that they were lies. Your own men there, when properly coerced, owned the hoax." He drew a slip of paper from his pocket and passed it around to the others.

"A man will admit anything under torture," said Varinka.

"Perhaps, but there is something else. Tonight you let a man escape us under a pretext. The *taichō* there did not stop him because your authority was higher than the *taichō*'s. This man, *Takeki*, is doubtless your partner. You are working for the *Shina-lin*, and anyone working for the Chinese is the enemy of Japan, therefore a traitor."

"But that proves nothing." said Varinka.

The officers looked at one another, smiling as men do when they have an ace as yet undisplayed. They looked back at Varinka. She was standing straight and steady. Her blue tunic with its high collar set off the brilliance of her yellow hair. But they saw nothing of her beauty. Not now.

"Tonight many men were killed," said the *taishō*. "And this has just been brought from the scene."

The man took the automatic she had given Kurt from his pocket and showed it to her.

"The number of this gun," said the *taishō*, "corresponds with the one issued to you. This is your gun. Some way you gave it to the foreigner. The final proof, *Takeki*, is that the men killed were members of Lin Wang's Death Squad. Their papers disclosed that to us. What more proof could you want?"

Heads moved from side to side. With an air of finality cigarettes were dropped to the floor and ground under boots.

"The sentence, *Takeki*, is death. A firing squad is being sent from the barracks. *Taichō* Shimazu, take this woman to the Wall. Bring back her head, so that there will be no tricks. That is all."

Varinka's expression did not change. She met their eyes unafraid.

From the street came the clank and measured tread of marching men. The sound stopped and the Japanese clambered into the truck. Two men stepped up to Varinka's side and took hold of her arms, *Taichō* Shimazu barked a command and went out through the entrance, followed by his prisoner.

"*Sayōnara, Takeki*," said the *taishō*. "Goodbye. I shall treasure your head."

Varinka did not look back. The guards thrust her into the car and sat down on either side. *Taichō* Shimazu took his place on one of the intermediate seats.

"Drive!" barked Shimazu to the silhouette of the driver.

The car started off. Varinka held her head erect, disdainful of the hands which held her fast.

An early dawn was coming up. The world was cold and thin as though seen through heavy gauze. The pearl shafts of the east did not reach far into the streets of Kalgan.

As the brightness grew, Chinese and Mongols on the streets turned to stare at the touring car followed by the truck full of soldiers. The sight was not new. This was obviously an execution party. Some luckless soul was about to add his death to the long list which paid for conquest.

Varinka looked straight ahead, chilly in her silk tunic, which fluttered a little in the brisk wind.

"Driver," said Shimazu, leaning forward, "this is not the way to the Wall. You are driving too fast."

Kurt smiled a triumphant smile. He had knocked out the driver and had hidden his body beside the wall of headquarters. In the darkness, with only his purloined military cap in evidence to those in the rear, he had easily escaped detection.

He stamped on the brakes and swung swiftly about, the blue-nosed .45 pointed generally at the three.

"*Tobi-dasu!*" cried Kurt. "Jump out! All of you!"

Varinka uttered a small cry of relief and surprise. The two bayoneted rifles swung forward. The soldiers would defend themselves and their prisoner at any cost. Kurt saw the flash of steel.

The captain snatched at his own automatic, fearless of death. Kurt caught the three separate movements and knew that he could not shoot fast enough. One of the three would get him.

But Varinka was not merely a spectator. In a swift movement she reached out with both hands and snatched the rifle barrels, holding them up for the instant which was needed.

The *taichō*'s gun flashed up. Kurt fired point-blank. Kurt reared up as the captain toppled to one side and caught the body by the shoulder. With a quick thrust he sent the *taichō* over the door and out.

The smoking muzzle of the .45 covered the other two Japanese. They let go their guns as though they were white hot. Varinka threw the weapons onto the floor of the car.

"*Tobi-dasu!*" cried Kurt again.

The two soldiers jumped away from Varinka and swung out precipitately.

The truck was coming up and the soldiers there had already seen the dead body of the captain on the ground. A rifle bullet ripped through the back window and bored a sparkling hole in the windshield.

Kurt threw the car in gear and stamped on the accelerator. The touring car lurched and gathered speed. Varinka crouched low. A slug ripped the tonneau over her head.

"Head south!" cried Varinka.

Kurt whipped the machine around a corner and raced out along a rough road. A gate was before them. Two guards, seeing the pursuit of the truck, stepped out with leveled rifles directly in front of the car.

Kurt jerked the wheel to the right and left. The Japanese jumped aside. The machine careened out through the twin towers and roared down a twisting road into China proper.

Varinka climbed over the back of the front seat and settled herself beside Kurt. She smiled at him.

He expected some kind of praise and was all ready to turn it aside. But she said, "I do not think that Anne Carsten could do that thing. I mean to catch the guns before they shoot."

Kurt stabbed her with a black-eyed glance, "Why bring her up?"

Varinka smiled and folded her hands upon her lap. She was sitting quite at ease, although the car plunged down a winding grade at sixty miles an hour.

"I thought," said Varinka, "that you loved her."

"Hell, no," said Kurt.

She looked disappointed. "But she is my friend."

Nothing about how he had gotten there, nothing, about what they would do or where they would go. Kurt snorted. Varinka sat there baiting him about love.

Wind whined through the hole in the windshield. The motor bellowed. Carts and droves of camels spilled off the road to make way for the juggernaut. The world was fully awake now, up and about its business. The morning sun yellowed the plain which stretched away from the hills deep into China.

The truck was far behind them, lost in dust, much too slow to keep pace with Kurt's masterful driving and the touring car's Western engine.

They rode for half an hour and then Varinka raised up to look behind them.

"They have gone now. Lucky, eh? You can turn at the next road and head east."

"East? That'll take us back into Japanese territory."

"You must head east," said Varinka. "I have business."

"Say, listen, haven't you had enough?"

"Oh, no. I must never leave unfinished business. Head east."

Grudgingly, Kurt turned down the road which was far worse than the one he left. He was beginning to think that Varinka was crazy.

He thought he knew it when the road started a little bit northeast. He was certain they would run into Japanese troops and the word would be telegraphed ahead of them. There would be no escape now.

But he didn't want to argue with the girl. He respected her too much.

They came to another crossroads and to a ruined stone tower whose stones strewed its base. Withered creepers clung forlornly to the cracked structure.

"Stop here and put the car behind this place," said Varinka.

"Stop here? What the devil do you want? What are you going to do?"

"Oh, I think very soon some Japanese will come along this other road in a car, heading east. How good are you with a rifle, my Kurt?"

"Good enough."

"Then take one of these and go behind that wall and when

the Japanese come, we shall see. After that we go further east, to a certain deserted fort."

Kurt knew it would be useless to argue with her. He parked the car, took one of the bayoneted rifles and got out. Dust was already rolling up along the other road.

"They come," said Varinka with a cat smile.

CHAPTER EIGHT

Lin Wang

KURT thrust the rifle through a loophole and slid off the safety catch. Varinka was standing beside him with the other weapon.

"I aim for the tires," said Varinka. "You aim for the driver. And don't let them get by!"

Kurt, although he did not understand the move, was quite ready to fix up any number of Japanese. The car was traveling straight toward them. The road bent around the old tower like an ox yoke.

Varinka fired and flipped out the smoking cartridge. Kurt aimed at the base of the windshield. His first and Varinka's second sounded as one explosion.

The machine yawed wildly. A pair of mustard-colored arms were flung out to one side. Dust and motion blurred the scene. The car seemed to trip over itself. It slid sideways toward a ditch, struck the embankment and went over, rolling, strewing men down the slope.

Kurt ran out, arriving at the top of the bank before any of the spilled occupants could move. The men were five in number, all of them Japanese.

But wait! A man-mountain was moving sluggishly to his feet. He turned and looked up and then bellowed a curse.

Captain Yang Ch'ieu sent wild fingers into his tunic for his automatic.

Dropping to one knee, Kurt leveled the rifle and sighted with the battle sight. He fired at Yang's chest. Yang roared and, waving his gun, began to run up the slope.

Kurt fired a second time and worked the bolt. Yang still came on, his flat face twisted with hate.

A third time Kurt sent a slug into the charging body, but he might as well have fired at the stones. Yang would not be stopped. With a sudden sense of panic, Kurt sent bullets four and five into the towering hulk.

Yang was a yard away from him. Yang was setting himself to fire and Kurt's magazine was empty.

Swinging the rifle about his head like a club, Kurt leaped up. The automatic flamed in his face, searing him with burning grains of powder.

Kurt dodged. He was off balance and falling. Yang, with a loud cry, depressed the muzzle of the automatic for the *coup de grâce*. Kurt cried out and rolled away, but there was no escaping that muzzle.

Suddenly Yang folded into himself. His tremendous body plunged rigid into the dust, sending up a swirling cloud. His fingers clawed at the ground. A look of surprise came over his face.

Wheeling, Kurt saw that Varinka was holding the three live Japanese motionless with the threat of her rifle. Her face was very strained. She had not dared deflect her attention from those armed men even for an instant.

Kurt looked back at Yang. The man was riddled. Every

bullet had plowed through the man mountain, three hitting vital spots. But the great vitality of the Chinese captain had scorned the mailed fist of death until the last. An ordinary man would have dropped under the first bullet.

"Tie them," said Varinka.

Kurt found cord and belts and laid the three Japanese in a neat row beside their smoking car. When he was finished, he saw that Varinka had fished a black satchel from the wreckage and was now holding it triumphantly.

"Come along," said Varinka, "I think, perhaps, that we have done a good job here." She looked thoughtful for a moment, and then said, "Wait. I think you had better take that officer's boots and cloak and cap."

Kurt did so without question. He pulled off his own shoes, tucked his pants into the boots, donned the cloak and the red-banded cap. "Now what?"

"I have one thing which they do not know," said Varinka. She pulled a telegraph blank from her tunic and showed it to him. "Lin Wang is waiting for us. The copy was brought to me by one of my men. Come, let us be going. It would be a crime to keep Lin Wang waiting."

Kurt began to have some vague idea of what this was all about. He slid in under the wheel and drove at an easy pace down the bumpy, deserted road, still heading east.

Varinka pulled a thick belt from her waist. "When we have gone a little way, you stop again."

He stopped and she showed him that she had phials of dye secreted in the belt—a part of a spy's equipment. She made him rub it on his face and hands. She fixed a small band behind his ears which pulled his eyes up at the corners, giving them a slant.

When she had made a presentable Japanese officer out of him, she crawled into the rear seat and laid down, spreading a robe over her.

"I am wanted. You are a staff officer. Drive on, my Kurt, and I will tell you when we get to Lin Wang's."

All through that day they made their way along the base of the hills which bound China on the north. They were skirting Japanese territory, but the Japanese would obviously expect them to head deep into China and take refuge there. They met no troops, only dull-faced Chinese and Mongols who were interested only in minding their own business in this bandit-ridden, war-torn land.

Kurt's nerves were on edge, but Varinka did not seem to mind. The tight tape about his head made his eyes smart, but that could not be helped. When dusk came at last he was very glad to stop.

"We are almost there," said Varinka. "Here at the right there is an old, deserted monastery. See it?"

Kurt did. The crumpled ruin looked desolate in the twilight, sprawling up a hillside. He nodded.

"The plan is short. Lin Wang is to die. We cannot kill him among his troops, that is impossible. You are to go to Lin Wang—dangerous, I know, but necessary—and tell him that Captain Yang and a *taishō* of the Japanese are waiting for a parley at this monastery. If Captain Yang is supposed to be there, then Lin Wang will suspect no plot and he will come.

Let him bring three or four soldiers if he wills. Tell him that the *taishō* is afraid to be seen going to Lin Wang.

"Lin Wang understands that this must be a secret affair and he'll be the last one to insist on a large bodyguard. He will come gladly and then . . . I suppose you will call it murder."

"I'll be very glad to see him dead," said Kurt.

"You follow them. When they come here, you get the guard. I'll get Lin Wang. His headquarters are about two miles down the road. Wait a while until I set the trap. Lead him straight up this road and to this entrance, then drop behind."

"Then . . ." said Kurt, "Lin Wang is selling out to the Japanese!"

"Right. He is a traitor to China and needs killing for the safety of the country. He sells his regimental support to Japan for the money which is in this black bag. There you have it."

"And you're not a Japanese spy?"

"No. I am a supporter of China. And the last duty I have is to kill Lin Wang. Go."

Kurt shook her hand and found that it trembled a little. She weaved close to him and he kissed her. She pushed him away toward Lin Wang's headquarters.

He took his time going, waiting until the evening meal would be over, letting Varinka set her trap. He had parked the car behind the monastery, ready for instant flight.

Once he heard a furtive movement behind him, but he could see nothing. When the darkness had fully closed in he changed his course and walked far off to the right of the road. That he might be going to his death did not bother him. He was marveling too much at Varinka's courage. To outwit a whole country and earn herself the name of *Takeki*, the Courageous!

When he came to the ancient fort he saw that guards were posted at the entrance, gray clad and very alert. But no other soldiers were about.

For a long time, nearly an hour, Kurt stayed in the shadows. He wanted to make certain that these two guards were the only men about the outside in case matters called for a hasty escape.

He was about to go down and announce himself when a small group came hurrying along the road. Two soldiers were dragging a third person, but from the distance, Kurt could not make out who that person was.

They came from the opposite direction from that which Kurt had taken, dispelling his fears that it might be Varinka. The three went past the guards and a door clanged shut behind them.

Kurt gripped his cloak tightly about him and with a purposeful stride, approached the two guards. His heart was hammering against his ribs, but he showed nothing of it in his face. He was too tall for a Japanese, he knew, but then some Japanese were tall.

The guards leveled their rifles at him. He made his Chinese crisp. "I am *Taichō* Shimazu, to see General Lin Wang on business."

They saw his cap and red band then and dropped their guns to their sides. One of them said, "He expects you, Captain."

That was easy enough. But maybe getting out would be another matter. Kurt kicked the door open and shut and, for some reason, thought locking it would be a good idea. Silently he dropped the chains in place. A moment later he heard a motor rumble outside and a squeal of brakes. That puzzled him, but it was too late to turn back now. If this was a Japanese officer . . .

He went on down the long, dimly lit hall, his boot-heels ringing and sending the echoes rocking emptily. He pushed open another door.

Lin Wang sat in a puddle of yellow light, flanked by two sentries. The rest of the room was dim. Great shadows flickered along the walls like crawling monsters about to pounce. Lin Wang was looking through candle flame at two soldiers and a prisoner.

Kurt was unnoticed. Something was familiar about the prisoner. Brown hair, slender shoulders. A military cape drooped down from the throat. The hair was disheveled.

Kurt almost cried out. He swallowed the sound and sagged against the door. The prisoner was Anne Carsten!

Lin Wang was speaking in English. His hands rattled before his twisted face. The black caverns criss-crossed his scaly visage and made his expression diabolical. His eyes were screwed up into black pinpoints, showing muddy blue flecks in the saffron light. When he spoke a small shower of scales fluttered to the desk.

"I have wanted to see you for some little time," said Lin Wang to Anne Carsten. "I once saw you coming out of a ballroom. You looked at me and shuddered and said to your companion that I was loathesome. Oh, I know how you felt. You are a beautiful woman. You could have the pick of men, but now the choice comes down to me. Tonight I am leaving China. As soon as a certain messenger—"

Anne shuddered and the ragged cape whispered against the floor. She was very white, but she held her chin up and looked coldly at Lin Wang.

Her voice was throaty. "Tonight you are leaving China. But I am not going with you. Try what you please, Lin Wang. I have ways of putting myself out of this world. In a necklace about my throat . . ." She clutched it. "I carry a swift poison." She pried the cover off. "One move and it goes down."

She had spoken too soon. The soldier beside her whipped it out of her hand. The broken golden chain slinked musically on the floor.

Lin Wang saw Kurt then. He looked up expectantly. "Pardon this, Captain. But a small side play. She is beautiful, don't you think?" He spoke in Japanese, out of courtesy.

"*Kirei na,*" said Kurt. "She is beautiful indeed—if you like white women. But this is not the time to speak of women." He felt a cold sweat starting out against his palms. Anne Carsten looked dazedly at him without a trace of recognition. After that first glance he had not dared to look at Anne.

"You have the money?" said Lin Wang. "Where is the *taishō?*"

"He is waiting for you. He was afraid to approach you direct. I will lead you to him."

"Very well, but here, sit down there in that chair and have

a glass of sake. I drink sake, now that I am to become wholly Japanese." He laughed at his joke and his fingers clattered against one another like a skeleton dancing. His hunched back shook.

"There is little time, *taishō*."

"Be not so impatient," replied Lin Wang irritably. "If I go now this woman may kill herself before I return."

Kurt chose a chair in the shadow and wrapped his cloak more tightly about him. A soldier handed him a glass of the hot red fluid.

Lin Wang was looking at Anne again. He licked his flaky lips. "Come, there's no need of wasting time. You have been brought here by my men. No one will ever know where you have gone. You might as well . . ." He stood up and came forward, moving one foot heavily along the floor, hitching himself along the edge of the desk, leaning heavily to the right.

Rifles and soldiers. Guards outside. Kurt sat very still. The liquor gagged him. He was looking at Anne again. She was not standing in very good light and he could not clearly see her face. Something was oddly wrong about her, something Kurt could not understand.

Rifles and soldiers. Kurt's hand slipped casually to his thigh and touched the butt of his .45. It was certain death, but . . . surely he couldn't do this thing and leave Varinka in the lurch. Once again he was confronted with the two women.

Lin Wang reached out with his queerly lifeless hand and patted Anne's cheek. She tried to wrench away, but the two soldiers held her securely. The men in the room were grinning.

"And you said I was loathesome. Oh, but you did. And if you didn't say it, I saw it in your eyes. It's there now. You think I am ugly, but I can be very pleasant. Very pleasant."

He pulled down a strand of her hair and stroked it. He hitched himself a little closer, looking up at her, head on one side, chuckling. Kurt remembered Bonner's fingernails. . . .

Something else was in the room which Kurt thought should not be there. He looked about restively. A black satchel stood beside the door. Lin Wang looked past Anne. He also saw the bag.

"And what did you bring for us there, my pretty?" said Lin Wang. He jerked his finger toward the bag, and a soldier stooped and picked it up. Lin Wang smiled at Anne. "Do not be impatient. We must get everything in order first."

Kurt froze. He felt dizzy.

Lin Wang forgot about the satchel then. He reached out and took hold of the top of Anne's cloak. With a quick jerk he ripped it away from her and threw it on the floor. Anne was wearing a blue tunic which was badly torn at the collar.

Lin Wang chuckled again. The soldier opened the bag. "Money! Japanese yen!" cried the soldier.

Lin Wang stared into the satchel and, then, with a roar wheeled about and, glared at Kurt. The money was there—and yet an officer had come to take him to a conference to give him the money. Lin Wang's wits worked well on one theme—treachery.

Kurt was up, back to the wall. "Duck!" he yelled.

The .45 came level through the slit of his cloak. Flame

stabbed from the jerking muzzle. Lead screamed from the walls only half stopped.

Lin Wang took two shots through his stomach. His clawing fingers contracted as he collapsed, twisting to one side. Screaming orders, he fell to the floor, instantly swallowed up by the flame and smoke and turmoil.

Kurt, without waiting for Lin Wang to go down, flung himself to the right. A rifle bullet missed him by fractions. He fired straight into a soldier's face, blasting out the whole jaw. He caught the man before he could go down, and holding the corpse before him as a shield, turned to meet the others.

He shot another. The room was a hell of deafening thunder and shrieks. The candles flickered serenely. A man rushed Kurt with a bayonet. Kurt dropped him.

Suddenly Kurt saw that only one soldier was on his feet. The Chinese charged, steel glittering, face distorted. Kurt heaved the bullet-torn corpse of his shield onto the point of the bayonet, stepped aside and pistoled the Chinese through the skull.

Anne turned Lin Wang over with her foot. She was smiling bitterly. Kurt snatched at her arm, but she would not go until she had grasped the satchel.

Thunder came from down the corridor where the entrance was chained shut. Men were trying to get in, and the sounds of voices indicated that their number was a dozen at least.

Kurt's automatic was empty. He pulled Anne up the hall and with a yell, began to work on the chains. Anne crouched in a niche in the wall.

"Come on!" cried Kurt in Chinese. "Your master is dying while you talk. In there, they will escape!"

Through the door surged the excited Chinese. They stopped for an instant to stare at Kurt.

"Traitors! Treason! They are killing him. Don't let them escape!"

The Chinese bolted down the corridor, wild-eyed at the thought that they might incur Lin Wang's wrath by flinching at duty—or even seeming to flinch.

When they had gone, Kurt snatched at Anne's hand and jerked her outside. He stopped, startled. Their car had been driven up before the gate. A truck, now empty, stood beside it. Gas cans were piled high on the chassis, as they always are in North China beyond the range of stations. Kurt snatched a pair of them and threw them into the touring car.

Anne climbed into the seat. Kurt slid under the wheel. Yells were coming from the old structure. The Chinese, realizing how thoroughly they had been duped, were coming back.

Anne hugged the satchel full of money, the price of a general's treason. Kurt sent the machine hurtling down the dark road. Shots rang sharply behind them, but the darkness was their mask.

"Then you . . ." said Kurt, "then you are both Anne Carsten and Varinka Savischna. But how . . . ?"

"Hollow capsules flatten the nose, pads raise the cheekbones. A yellow wig hides brown hair. Pads broaden shoulders. Heels can be high or low. A voice and accent are nothing to be changed." She laughed and leaned against him. "I was good. I even had you fooled. You didn't know what to think when

Anne Carsten asked you about Varinka and Varinka asked you about Anne. They are both the same.

"But your piggish answers were balanced tonight. I thought they would know sooner than they did. But they are very dull, those fellows. They saw us come, I suppose, and two soldiers surprised me. A third caught me from behind, and I could do nothing. They took our car and missed the way. In the dark they didn't see me remove my disguise. If Varinka were caught, that would be terrible. But Anne Carsten wouldn't be so suddenly deceased.

"How I waited for you to come in there! And you came so beautifully, too. Even I was fooled." She paused for a little while, watching to see that they were far outdistancing their pursuit. Then she sighed and pressed closer to him. "My job is over. I've killed Lin Wang, or seen him killed, as I said I would after he murdered my father, but I never could have, had it not been for you.

"I'm free now, I'm not serving the powers of China any more. I advised them three days ago that Lin Wang was a traitor. He knew I would do that. Oh, how he wanted me killed! He knew what I was as Varinka, and he knew the Japanese thought I was a spy. . . . But there, it's all done and put aside and we never have to say where we got all this money. We've earned it. We're free, and at peace with the world. The Japanese will never know that Varinka is Anne Carsten."

"Free?" said Kurt. "Free? Good God, I still face a murder charge in Shanghai!"

"Oh, that? Why, forget it, sweetness—just forget it." She

reached into her tunic and pulled out the confession, handing it to him. He glanced at it by the light of the dash and saw that it was real.

"But how . . . ?" said Kurt.

"I took it out of Lin Wang's jacket while you were busy thinking about target practice in the room. I had to get all of his papers, but—"

She never finished the sentence. In spite of the hurtling speed of their machine, in spite of the bumps in the road, Kurt cut her short with a good, solid, brutal kiss.

Story Preview

Story Preview

NOW that you've just ventured through one of the captivating tales in the Stories from the Golden Age collection by L. Ron Hubbard, turn the page and enjoy a preview of *Orders Is Orders*. Join Marine Gunnery Sergeant James Mitchell and Private First Class Spivits, assigned to brave a 200-mile trek to bring cholera serum to a remote American consulate in Shunkien, China in a treacherous mission set against impossible odds—because they must reach the trapped Americans caught in the crossfire of the invading Japanese forces.

Orders Is Orders

THE doomed city of Shunkien poured flame-torn billows of smoke skyward to hide the sun. Mile after square mile spread the smoldering expanse of crumbling walls and corpse-littered streets.

And still from the Peking area came the bombers of the Rising Sun to further wreck the ruins. Compact squadrons scudding through the pall of greasy smoke turned, dived, zoomed, leaving black mushrooms swiftly growing behind their racing shadows.

Along a high bluff to the north of town, a line of artillery emplacements belched flame and thunder, and mustard-colored men ministered to their plunging guns.

Japan was pounding wreckage into ashes, wiping out a city which had thrived since the time of Genghis Khan, obliterating a railhead to prevent further concentration of Chinese legions.

Down amid the erupting shambles, three regiments of Chinese troops held on, bellies to dust behind barricades of paving stones, sandbags and barbed wire, shoulders wedged into the embrasures of the cracking walls, intent brown eyes to antiaircraft sights in the uprooted railway station.

They fought because they could not retreat. Two hundred miles and two Japanese army corps stood between them and the sea. Somewhere out in the once-fertile plains two Chinese armies groped for the enemy. But the battle lines were everywhere, running parallel to nothing, a huge labyrinth of war engines and marching legions.

There was no hope for Shunkien. Once proud signs protruded from the rubble which overlaid the gutters. The thoroughfares were dotted with the unburied dead, men and women and children. Thicker were these ragged bundles near the south gate where lines of refugees had striven to leave the town, only to be blasted down at the very exit.

The cannonading was a deafening monotone. The smoke and dust drifted and entwined. Walls wearily slid outward, slowly at first, then faster to crash with a roar, making an echo to the thunder of artillery along the ridge.

War was here, with Famine on the right and Death upon the left and Pestilence riding rear guard to make the sweep complete.

In the center of the city, close by a boulevard now gutted with shell holes and clogged with wrecked trolleys and automobiles and inert bodies, stood the United States Consulate.

The gates were tightly closed and the walls were still intact and high above, on a tall flagstaff, buffeted by the concussion of shells, Old Glory stood brightly out against the darkness of the smoke.

The building was small and the corridors were jammed with the hundred and sixteen Americans who had taken refuge there. Without baggage, glad enough to be still alive, they sat in groups and nursed their cigarettes and grinned and cracked jokes and made bets on their chances of being missed by all the shells which came shrieking down into the town.

It was hard to talk above the ceaseless roar, but they talked. Talked of Hoboken and Sioux City and Denver and argued the superior merits of their towns. Though their all was invested in and about Shunkien, though most of them had not been home for years, Frisco and Chi and the Big Town furnished the whole of their conversation.

A baby was crying and its white-faced mother tried to sing above the cataract of sound which beat against the walls outside. A machinery salesman tore his linen handkerchief into small bits and stuffed fragments of it into the child's ears. Thankfully, it stopped whimpering and the mother smiled and the salesman, suddenly finding himself caught, moved hurriedly away before he could be thanked.

Within the consular office, the consul, Thomas Jackson, moved to the side of his radio operator. Jackson was white-haired, small, nervous of face and hands. He looked at the expanse of gleaming dials as though trying to read hope in their metal faces.

The operator, a youth scarcely out of his teens, leaned over a key and rattled it. He threw a switch and pressed the earphones against his head. He lighted a cigarette with nicotine-stained fingers and stuck it in his mouth. He pulled a typewriter to him and began to write.

"I've got Shanghai again, sir," said the operator. "They want to know how we're holding out."

"Tell them we're all right so far, and God knows we've been lucky." Jackson leaned close to the operator and then glanced around to see that no one else in the room could hear. "Tell them for the love of God to get the cholera antitoxin to us if they expect to find any of us alive after this is over. Tell them Asiatic cholera is certain to follow, has already begun. And then tell them that we've got to have money—gold. Our checks and paper are no good and the food is running low."

The young operator precariously perched his cigarette on the already burned edge of his table and began to make the bug click and quiver.

A few minutes later he beckoned to the consul. "They say the USS *Miami* is already proceeding down the coast with both the serum and the money."

"Damned little good that will do us," moaned Jackson. "A cruiser can't come two hundred miles inland."

"They said they'd try to get it through to us, sir. They want to know how long we can hold out."

Jackson ran bony fingers through his awry white hair and looked around him. He singled out a fat little man whose eyes were so deep in his head they could not be seen at all.

"Doctor," said Jackson, loud enough to be heard above the cannonade but not loud enough for anyone else to overhear, "Doctor, how long do you think we can last without the cholera shots?"

"With corpses strewn from Hell to Halifax?" puffed the doctor. "Now, tomorrow, next week, maybe never."

"Please," begged the consul, "you're not staking your reputation on this. How long will it take?"

"The reports are," said the doctor, "that it is just now starting to spread. I'll give it five days to reach here because, in five days, we'll have to start going out to buy food—if we can find the gold with which to buy it. Otherwise, we stay here bottled up, boil our water and starve to death. We all had cholera shots before we came into this area, but they won't prove effective unless bolstered with secondary, epidemic shots. If we get that serum here before Saturday, there's a chance of our living—as far as disease is concerned—through this mess. But mind you, now, you can't quote me. Anything is liable to happen."

"Thanks," said Jackson gratefully.

The consul went back to the youth at the key. "Tell them it's got to be here by Saturday, Billy. Not a day later. Though how they'll get it here, only God himself can tell."

He looked out through the office door into the outside passageway where a hundred and more Americans tried to take it calmly. The floor of the consulate was shaking as though a procession of huge trucks rumbled deafeningly by.

To find out more about *Orders Is Orders* and how you can obtain your copy, go to www.goldenagestories.com.

Glossary

STORIES FROM THE GOLDEN AGE *reflect the words and expressions used in the 1930s and 1940s, adding unique flavor and authenticity to the tales. While a character's speech may often reflect regional origins, it also can convey attitudes common in the day. So that readers can better grasp such cultural and historical terms, uncommon words or expressions of the era, the following glossary has been provided.*

---

amah: (in India and the Far East) a female servant; maid.

bead on, drew a: took careful aim at. This term alludes to the *bead*, a small metal knob on a firearm used as a front sight.

belaying pin: a large wooden or metal pin that fits into a hole in a rail on a ship or boat, and to which a rope can be fastened.

bichloride of mercury: a water-soluble and deadly poisonous crystalline solid used for such things as embalming, to preserve wood, and to kill germs, insects and rodents. It is also a useful but dangerous antiseptic. To help distinguish it as poisonous when being dispensed as a topical antiseptic, it is in the form of blue angular-shaped tablets.

Big Town: nickname for New York City.

bucko: a person who is domineering and bullying.

bucko mate: the mate of a sailing ship who drives his crew by the power of his fists.

Bund: the word *bund* means an embankment and "the Bund" refers to a particular stretch of embanked riverfront along the Huangpu River in Shanghai that is lined with dozens of historical buildings. The Bund lies north of the old walled city of Shanghai. This was initially a British settlement; later the British and American settlements were combined into the International Settlement. A building boom at the end of the nineteenth century and beginning of the twentieth century led to the Bund becoming a major financial hub of East Asia.

Chi: Chicago.

cholera: an infectious disease of the small intestine, typically contracted from infected water.

chow bench: a short round table with four stools that fit underneath it.

clothes press: a piece of furniture for storing clothes, with hanging space and sometimes drawers or shelves.

Colt .45: a .45-caliber automatic pistol manufactured by the Colt Firearms Company of Hartford, Connecticut. Colt was founded by Samuel Colt (1814–1862), who revolutionized the firearms industry.

Concession: something conceded by a government or a controlling authority, as a grant of land, a privilege or a franchise. In Shanghai, there was land set aside by treaty as a spot where foreigners could live and trade, which is referred to as the Concession; otherwise known as "the Bund."

coup de grâce: (French) a finishing stroke.

cutter: a ship's boat, powered by a motor or oars and used for transporting stores or passengers.

down in the mouth: dejected; depressed; disheartened.

embrasures: (in fortification) openings, as a loophole through which missiles may be discharged.

Frisco: San Francisco.

Genghis Khan: (1162?–1227) Mongol conqueror who founded the largest land empire in history and whose armies, known for their use of terror, conquered many territories and slaughtered the populations of entire cities.

G-men: government men; agents of the Federal Bureau of Investigation.

gunwale: the upper edge of the side of a boat. Originally a gunwale was a platform where guns were mounted, and was designed to accommodate the additional stresses imposed by the artillery being used.

hard-boiled: tough and cynical.

Hell to Halifax: a variation of the phrase "from here to Halifax," meaning everywhere, in all places no matter how far from here. "Halifax" is a county in eastern Canada, on the Atlantic Ocean.

Huangpu: long river in China flowing through Shanghai. It divides the city into two regions.

Kalgan: a city in northeast China near the Great Wall that served as both a commercial and a military center. Kalgan means "gate in a barrier" or "frontier" in Mongolian. It is the eastern entry into China from Inner Mongolia.

kirei na: (Japanese) beautiful.

mailed fist: superior force.

merchant prince: an extremely wealthy, powerful and prestigious merchant.

Mikado: the emperor of Japan; a title no longer used.

Nō: (Japanese) classic drama of Japan, developed chiefly in the fourteenth century, employing verse, prose, choral song and dance in highly conventionalized formal and thematic patterns derived from religious sources and folk myths.

Old Glory: a common nickname for the flag of the US, bestowed by William Driver (1803–1886), an early nineteenth-century American sea captain. Given the flag as a gift, he hung it from his ship's mast and hailed it as "Old Glory" when he left harbor for a trip around the world (1831–1832) as commander of a whaling vessel. Old Glory served as the ship's official flag throughout the voyage.

Peking: now Beijing, China.

postern: a small gate or entrance at the back of a building, especially a castle or a fort.

rapier: a small sword, especially of the eighteenth century, having a narrow blade and used for thrusting.

Rising Sun: Japan; the characters that make up Japan's name mean "the sun's origin," which is why Japan is sometimes identified as the "Land of the Rising Sun." It is also the military flag of Japan and was used as the ensign of the Imperial Japanese Navy and the war flag of the Imperial Japanese Army until the end of World War II.

sampan: any of various small boats of the Far East, as one propelled by a single oar over the stern and provided with a roofing of mats.

sayō: (Japanese) yes; indeed; that's right.

sayōnara: (Japanese) goodbye.

Scheherazade: the female narrator of *The Arabian Nights,* who during one thousand and one adventurous nights saved her life by entertaining her husband, the king, with stories.

scimitar: a curved, single-edged sword of Oriental origin.

sculling oar: single oar that is moved from side to side at the stern of a boat to propel it forward.

Shanghai: city of eastern China at the mouth of the Yangtze River, and the largest city in the country. Shanghai was opened to foreign trade by treaty in 1842 and quickly prospered. France, Great Britain and the United States all held large concessions (rights to use land granted by a government) in the city until the early twentieth century.

Shina-lin: (Japanese) Chinese officials.

SS: steamship.

taichō: (Japanese) leader of a small group.

taishō: (Japanese) colonel.

Tobi-dasu!: (Japanese) Jump out!

tomodachi: (Japanese) friend; companion.

tonneau: a waterproof cover, generally of canvas or vinyl, that can be fastened over the cockpit of a roadster or convertible to protect the interior.

tramp: a freight vessel that does not run regularly between fixed ports, but takes a cargo wherever shippers desire.

tsumesho: (Japanese) guard room.

USS: United States Ship.

White Russian: a Russian who opposed the Bolsheviks (Russian Communist Party).

yakunin: (Japanese) government official.

Yellow Sea: an arm of the Pacific Ocean between the Chinese mainland and the Korean Peninsula. It connects with the East China Sea to the south.

L. Ron Hubbard
in the Golden Age
of Pulp Fiction

*In writing an adventure story
a writer has to know that he is adventuring
for a lot of people who cannot.
The writer has to take them here and there
about the globe and show them
excitement and love and realism.
As long as that writer is living the part of an
adventurer when he is hammering
the keys, he is succeeding with his story.*

*Adventuring is a state of mind.
If you adventure through life, you have a
good chance to be a success on paper.*

*Adventure doesn't mean globe-trotting,
exactly, and it doesn't mean great deeds.
Adventuring is like art.
You have to live it to make it real.*

— *L. RON HUBBARD*

L. Ron Hubbard
and American
Pulp Fiction

B ORN March 13, 1911, L. Ron Hubbard lived a life at
least as expansive as the stories with which he enthralled
a hundred million readers through a fifty-year career.

Originally hailing from Tilden, Nebraska, he spent his
formative years in a classically rugged Montana, replete with
the cowpunchers, lawmen and desperadoes who would later
people his Wild West adventures. And lest anyone imagine
those adventures were drawn from vicarious experience, he
was not only breaking broncs at a tender age, he was also
among the few whites ever admitted into Blackfoot society
as a bona fide blood brother. While if only to round out an
otherwise rough and tumble youth, his mother was that rarity
of her time—a thoroughly educated woman—who introduced
her son to the classics of Occidental literature even before
his seventh birthday.

But as any dedicated L. Ron Hubbard reader will attest, his
world extended far beyond Montana. In point of fact, and as the
son of a United States naval officer, by the age of eighteen he
had traveled over a quarter of a million miles. Included therein
were three Pacific crossings to a then still mysterious Asia, where
he ran with the likes of Her British Majesty's agent-in-place

L. Ron Hubbard, left, at Congressional Airport, Washington, DC, 1931, with members of George Washington University flying club.

for North China, and the last in the line of Royal Magicians from the court of Kublai Khan. For the record, L. Ron Hubbard was also among the first Westerners to gain admittance to forbidden Tibetan monasteries below Manchuria, and his photographs of China's Great Wall long graced American geography texts.

Upon his return to the United States and a hasty completion of his interrupted high school education, the young Ron Hubbard entered George Washington University. There, as fans of his aerial adventures may have heard, he earned his wings as a pioneering barnstormer at the dawn of American aviation. He also earned a place in free-flight record books for the longest sustained flight above Chicago. Moreover, as a roving reporter for *Sportsman Pilot* (featuring his first professionally penned articles), he further helped inspire a generation of pilots who would take America to world airpower.

Immediately beyond his sophomore year, Ron embarked on the first of his famed ethnological expeditions, initially to then untrammeled Caribbean shores (descriptions of which would later fill a whole series of West Indies mystery-thrillers). That the Puerto Rican interior would also figure into the future of Ron Hubbard stories was likewise no accident. For in addition to cultural studies of the island, a 1932–33

LRH expedition is rightly remembered as conducting the first complete mineralogical survey of a Puerto Rico under United States jurisdiction.

There was many another adventure along this vein: As a lifetime member of the famed Explorers Club, L. Ron Hubbard charted North Pacific waters with the first shipboard radio direction finder, and so pioneered a long-range navigation system universally employed until the late twentieth century. While not to put too fine an edge on it, he also held a rare Master Mariner's license to pilot any vessel, of any tonnage in any ocean.

Yet lest we stray too far afield, there is an LRH note at this juncture in his saga, and it reads in part:

"I started out writing for the pulps, writing the best I knew, writing for every mag on the stands, slanting as well as I could."

To which one might add: His earliest submissions date from the summer of 1934, and included tales drawn from true-to-life Asian adventures, with characters roughly modeled on British/American intelligence operatives he had known in Shanghai. His early Westerns were similarly peppered with details drawn from personal experience. Although therein lay a first hard lesson from the often cruel world of the pulps. His first Westerns were soundly rejected as lacking the authenticity of a Max Brand yarn

Capt. L. Ron Hubbard in Ketchikan, Alaska, 1940, on his Alaskan Radio Experimental Expedition, the first of three voyages conducted under the Explorers Club flag.

(a particularly frustrating comment given L. Ron Hubbard's Westerns came straight from his Montana homeland, while Max Brand was a mediocre New York poet named Frederick Schiller Faust, who turned out implausible six-shooter tales from the terrace of an Italian villa).

Nevertheless, and needless to say, L. Ron Hubbard persevered and soon earned a reputation as among the most publishable names in pulp fiction, with a ninety percent placement rate of first-draft manuscripts. He was also among the most prolific, averaging between seventy and a hundred thousand words a month. Hence the rumors that L. Ron Hubbard had redesigned a typewriter for faster keyboard action and pounded out manuscripts on a continuous roll of butcher paper to save the precious seconds it took to insert a single sheet of paper into manual typewriters of the day.

That all L. Ron Hubbard stories did not run beneath said byline is yet another aspect of pulp fiction lore. That is, as publishers periodically rejected manuscripts from top-drawer authors if only to avoid paying top dollar, L. Ron Hubbard and company just as frequently replied with submissions under various pseudonyms. In Ron's case, the

---

A MAN OF MANY NAMES

Between 1934 and 1950, L. Ron Hubbard authored more than fifteen million words of fiction in more than two hundred classic publications. To supply his fans and editors with stories across an array of genres and pulp titles, he adopted fifteen pseudonyms in addition to his already renowned L. Ron Hubbard byline.

Winchester Remington Colt
Lt. Jonathan Daly
Capt. Charles Gordon
Capt. L. Ron Hubbard
Bernard Hubbel
Michael Keith
Rene Lafayette
Legionnaire 148
Legionnaire 14830
Ken Martin
Scott Morgan
Lt. Scott Morgan
Kurt von Rachen
Barry Randolph
Capt. Humbert Reynolds

---

list included: Rene Lafayette, Captain Charles Gordon, Lt. Scott Morgan and the notorious Kurt von Rachen—supposedly on the lam for a murder rap, while hammering out two-fisted prose in Argentina. The point: While L. Ron Hubbard as Ken Martin spun stories of Southeast Asian intrigue, LRH as Barry Randolph authored tales of

romance on the Western range—which, stretching between a dozen genres is how he came to stand among the two hundred elite authors providing close to a million tales through the glory days of American Pulp Fiction.

L. Ron Hubbard, circa 1930, at the outset of a literary career that would finally span half a century.

In evidence of exactly that, by 1936 L. Ron Hubbard was literally leading pulp fiction's elite as president of New York's American Fiction Guild. Members included a veritable pulp hall of fame: Lester "Doc Savage" Dent, Walter "The Shadow" Gibson, and the legendary Dashiell Hammett—to cite but a few.

Also in evidence of just where L. Ron Hubbard stood within his first two years on the American pulp circuit: By the spring of 1937, he was ensconced in Hollywood, adopting a Caribbean thriller for Columbia Pictures, remembered today as *The Secret of Treasure Island*. Comprising fifteen thirty-minute episodes, the L. Ron Hubbard screenplay led to the most profitable matinée serial in Hollywood history. In accord with Hollywood culture, he was thereafter continually called upon

The 1937 Secret of Treasure Island, *a fifteen-episode serial adapted for the screen by L. Ron Hubbard from his novel,* Murder at Pirate Castle.

to rewrite/doctor scripts—most famously for long-time friend and fellow adventurer Clark Gable.

In the interim—and herein lies another distinctive chapter of the L. Ron Hubbard story—he continually worked to open Pulp Kingdom gates to up-and-coming authors. Or, for that matter, anyone who wished to write. It was a fairly unconventional stance, as markets were already thin and competition razor sharp. But the fact remains, it was an L. Ron Hubbard hallmark that he vehemently lobbied on behalf of young authors—regularly supplying instructional articles to trade journals, guest-lecturing to short story classes at George Washington University and Harvard, and even founding his own creative writing competition. It was established in 1940, dubbed the Golden Pen, and guaranteed winners both New York representation and publication in *Argosy*.

But it was John W. Campbell Jr.'s *Astounding Science Fiction* that finally proved the most memorable LRH vehicle. While every fan of L. Ron Hubbard's galactic epics undoubtedly knows the story, it nonetheless bears repeating: By late 1938, the pulp publishing magnate of Street & Smith was determined to revamp *Astounding Science Fiction* for broader readership. In particular, senior editorial director F. Orlin Tremaine called for stories with a stronger *human element*. When acting editor John W. Campbell balked, preferring his spaceship-driven tales, Tremaine enlisted Hubbard. Hubbard, in turn, replied with the genre's first truly *character-driven* works, wherein heroes are pitted not against bug-eyed monsters but the mystery and majesty of deep space itself—and thus was launched the Golden Age of Science Fiction.

The names alone are enough to quicken the pulse of any science fiction aficionado, including LRH friend and protégé, Robert Heinlein, Isaac Asimov, A. E. van Vogt and Ray Bradbury. Moreover, when coupled with LRH stories of fantasy, we further come to what's rightly been described as the foundation of every modern tale of horror: L. Ron Hubbard's immortal *Fear.* It was rightly proclaimed by Stephen King as one of the very few works to genuinely warrant that overworked term "classic"—as in: *"This is a classic tale of creeping, surreal menace and horror. . . . This is one of the really, really good ones."*

L. Ron Hubbard, 1948, among fellow science fiction luminaries at the World Science Fiction Convention in Toronto.

To accommodate the greater body of L. Ron Hubbard fantasies, Street & Smith inaugurated *Unknown*—a classic pulp if there ever was one, and wherein readers were soon thrilling to the likes of *Typewriter in the Sky* and *Slaves of Sleep* of which Frederik Pohl would declare: *"There are bits and pieces from Ron's work that became part of the language in ways that very few other writers managed."*

And, indeed, at J. W. Campbell Jr.'s insistence, Ron was regularly drawing on themes from the Arabian Nights and so introducing readers to a world of genies, jinn, Aladdin and Sinbad—all of which, of course, continue to float through cultural mythology to this day.

At least as influential in terms of post-apocalypse stories was L. Ron Hubbard's 1940 *Final Blackout*. Generally acclaimed as the finest anti-war novel of the decade and among the ten best works of the genre ever authored—here, too, was a tale that would live on in ways few other writers imagined.

Portland, Oregon, 1943; L. Ron Hubbard, captain of the US Navy subchaser PC 815.

Hence, the later Robert Heinlein verdict: "Final Blackout *is as perfect a piece of science fiction as has ever been written.*"

Like many another who both lived and wrote American pulp adventure, the war proved a tragic end to Ron's sojourn in the pulps. He served with distinction in four theaters and was highly decorated for commanding corvettes in the North Pacific. He was also grievously wounded in combat, lost many a close friend and colleague and thus resolved to say farewell to pulp fiction and devote himself to what it had supported these many years—namely, his serious research.

But in no way was the LRH literary saga at an end, for as he wrote some thirty years later, in 1980:

"Recently there came a period when I had little to do. This was novel in a life so crammed with busy years, and I decided to amuse myself by writing a novel that was pure *science fiction."*

That work was *Battlefield Earth: A Saga of the Year 3000*. It was an immediate *New York Times* bestseller and, in fact, the first international science fiction blockbuster in decades. It was not, however, L. Ron Hubbard's magnum opus, as that distinction is generally reserved for his next and final work: The 1.2 million word *Mission Earth*.

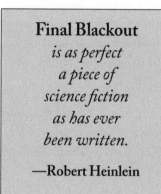

Final Blackout
is as perfect a piece of science fiction as has ever been written.

—Robert Heinlein

How he managed those 1.2 million words in just over twelve months is yet another piece of the L. Ron Hubbard legend. But the fact remains, he did indeed author a ten-volume *dekalogy* that lives in publishing history for the fact that each and every volume of the series was also a *New York Times* bestseller.

Moreover, as subsequent generations discovered L. Ron Hubbard through republished works and novelizations of his screenplays, the mere fact of his name on a cover signaled an international bestseller. . . . Until, to date, sales of his works exceed hundreds of millions, and he otherwise remains among the most enduring and widely read authors in literary history. Although as a final word on the tales of L. Ron Hubbard, perhaps it's enough to simply reiterate what editors told readers in the glory days of American Pulp Fiction:

He writes the way he does, brothers, because he's been there, seen it and done it!

THE STORIES FROM THE GOLDEN AGE

Your ticket to adventure starts here with the Stories from
the Golden Age collection by master storyteller L. Ron Hubbard.
These gripping tales are set in a kaleidoscope of exotic locales and brim
with fascinating characters, including some of the
most vile villains, dangerous dames and brazen heroes
you'll ever get to meet.

The entire collection of over one hundred and fifty stories is being
released in a series of eighty books and audiobooks.
For an up-to-date listing of available titles,
go to www.goldenagestories.com.

AIR ADVENTURE

FAR-FLUNG ADVENTURE

The Adventure of "X"
All Frontiers Are Jealous
The Barbarians
The Black Sultan
Black Towers to Danger
The Bold Dare All
Buckley Plays a Hunch
The Cossack
Destiny's Drum
Escape for Three
Fifty-Fifty O'Brien
The Headhunters
Hell's Legionnaire
He Walked to War
Hostage to Death

Hurricane
The Iron Duke
Machine Gun 21,000
Medals for Mahoney
Price of a Hat
Red Sand
The Sky Devil
The Small Boss of Nunaloha
The Squad That Never Came Back
Starch and Stripes
Tomb of the Ten Thousand Dead
Trick Soldier
While Bugles Blow!
Yukon Madness

SEA ADVENTURE

Cargo of Coffins
The Drowned City
False Cargo
Grounded
Loot of the Shanung
Mister Tidwell, Gunner

The Phantom Patrol
Sea Fangs
Submarine
Twenty Fathoms Down
Under the Black Ensign

TALES FROM THE ORIENT

MYSTERY

FANTASY

Borrowed Glory
The Crossroads
Danger in the Dark
The Devil's Rescue
He Didn't Like Cats

If I Were You
The Last Drop
The Room
The Tramp

SCIENCE FICTION

The Automagic Horse
Battle of Wizards
Battling Bolto
The Beast
Beyond All Weapons
A Can of Vacuum
The Conroy Diary
The Dangerous Dimension
Final Enemy
The Great Secret
Greed
The Invaders

A Matter of Matter
The Obsolete Weapon
One Was Stubborn
The Planet Makers
The Professor Was a Thief
The Slaver
Space Can
Strain
Tough Old Man
240,000 Miles Straight Up
When Shadows Fall

WESTERN